SHADOW
OF THE
WALL

He was just about to shake his sleeve over the bag's gaping mouth when the larger of the two youths gave a yell.

"My God, that's Michal Edelman. Stinking little Yid. I'd recognize him anywhere." Misha looked into the youth's face for just an instant, but long enough to recognize the elder brother of a boy who used to be in his class at school. He had always been a bully; Misha remembered how he had been one of the ringleaders of Jewhunts and Jewbaiting games even then.

"What the hell are you doing here, you filthy Jewscum?" he roared.

Misha didn't wait to hear more. Dropping the apples, he turned and fled, as unaware of direction and destination as of the ache in his leg. He was mindful only of the shouts and steps behind him, which seemed to be almost on his heels.

CHRISTA LAIRD

SHADOW
OF THE
WALL

A Beech Tree Paperback Book
New York

The Library of Congress has cataloged the Greenwillow Books edition of
Shadow of the Wall as follows:
Laird, Christa.
Shadow of the wall/Christa Laird.
p. cm.
Summary: Living with his mother and two sisters in the Warsaw Ghetto,
Misha is befriended by the director of the orphanage, Dr. Korczak, and finds
a purpose to his life when he joins a resistance organization.
ISBN 0-688-09336-1
1. Holocaust, Jewish (1939–1945)—Poland—Warsaw—Juvenile fiction.
[1. Holocaust, Jewish (1939–1945)—Poland—Warsaw—Fiction. 2. Jews—
Poland—Warsaw—Fiction.
3. Korczak, Janusz, 1878–1942—Fiction.
4. World War, 1939–1945—Poland—Warsaw—Fiction.
5. Poland—History—Occupation, 1939–1945—Fiction.] I. Title.
PZ7.L1577Sh 1990 [Fic]—dc20 89-34469 CIP AC

1 3 5 7 9 10 8 6 4 2
First Beech Tree Edition, 1997
ISBN 0-688-15291-0

FOR
MY
FATHER
RUDOLF JULIUS FALCK
1920 – 1944

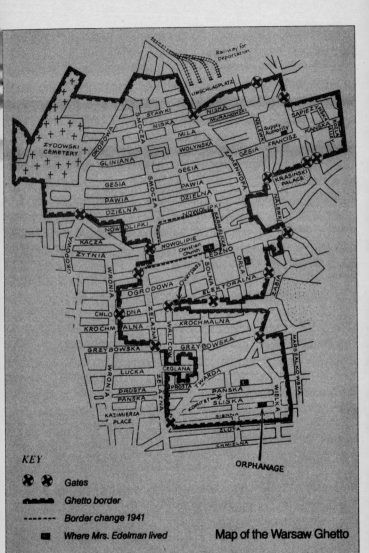

KEY

⊗ ⊗	Gates
▬▬▬	Ghetto border
-------	Border change 1941
■	Where Mrs. Edelman lived

ORPHANAGE

Map of the Warsaw Ghetto

CHAPTER 1

WHEN MISHA FIRST HEARD the sound of marching, he was still some distance from the orphanage. He imagined the boots: black bully boots. He pressed himself into the dark shadow of the wall and waited, holding his breath as if afraid that the very bricks might betray his presence. When he did dare to turn his head and look up Zelazna Street, he could see for at least ninety meters, despite the failing light. There indeed were the men in boots: four SS men in two pairs, followed closely by two members of the blue-clad Polish police. A harsh and abrupt call rang out; the marching came to an equally abrupt stop. The two blue policemen at the rear fell out of the formation and walked up some steps to a front door. Misha narrowed his eyes in a frenzy of concentration. *Who* lived at that house? Who *was* it? As if to help him remember, a quick succession of shouts rang out; the two blue policemen disappeared into the house and reappeared almost immediately with two of its occupants. Misha squeezed his eyes tight closed, trying to shut out the identity of those two people until, seconds later, some devil curiosity made him open them again.

The man who was being torn from his home within Misha's full and helpless view was Honek Bergson, the baker, together with his elder son, Marek. Misha knew them both, not well, but he had good reason to remember them kindly. Nearly eighteen months ago, at the end of October 1940, when Misha and his family were preparing to leave for the ghetto—or "Jewish quarter," as the Nazis called it—they had been unable to cram all the belongings they needed into their two handcarts. Honek, who was a widower, and his two sons had passed just as Rachel's dollhouse was about to be jettisoned, and they managed to find a corner for it in one of their own carts. Rachel, delighted, had almost skipped into the ghetto.

But now father and son were pushed across the street and made to stand, hands above their heads, facing the outer ghetto wall; they were frisked by the Polish policemen who then, under barked orders, stood aside. The SS men turned ninety degrees in the street like some black four-headed monster and then, quite literally before Misha realized what was happening, the baker and the eighteen-year-old boy slumped simultaneously to the ground as a volley of shots punctured the murky ghetto dusk.

Misha clenched his fists so hard that they began to hurt. He barely noticed the black monster turn through another ninety degrees and beat its rhythmic retreat. In the last two and a half years, since the old familiar Warsaw had begun to tumble down around him, Misha had been through most human feelings. There had been sheer physical panic at the man-made thunder and lightning that, unlike God's, seemed to leave no comforting space for counting in-between; there had been hunger, the sort that made the lining of your stomach burn at the sight of someone else's loaf of bread; the strange feelings when baby Elena was born, which no public labels seemed to fit and so ought perhaps to be disowned; piercing sadness when his father died from typhus fever last September; and the gnawing, nameless "thing" at his very center that stirred in its shallow sleep when his emaciated mother had a coughing spasm.

Could there be much more for a boy not yet fourteen to endure? It wasn't that Misha was given to self-pity; that was something that neither his character nor those around him would allow. It was simply that he doubted his own strength to cope with much more, and that strength had at all costs to be maintained: Three other people besides himself counted on it.

Then, without warning, Misha did feel something entirely new. As he stared up the street at the little heap the men in boots had left behind, his blood ran suddenly black with wrath. It was an oddly exhilarating sensation, and Misha knew without doubt that it came from God. In that moment of glorious omnipotent rage, the gentle baker and his son were transformed for Misha into archangels. He vowed in silent fervor to avenge their murders, and, in so doing, to avenge all the other pitiless things that had spread their stain across his childhood.

A few moments later, with a strange new calm in his heart, Misha continued his journey back to the orphanage. When their father had fallen ill the previous summer, their mother, already very weak and fearful for her children's survival, had begged Doctor Korczak to consider taking them into the Orphans' Home, though they were not actually orphans. "They're bad times," Misha remembered her saying sadly, "when a mother puts her children into an institution out of love."

Doctor Korczak, who had brought up Misha's own father after he had been orphaned, welcomed these three "grandchildren," as he called them, with his shy, gentle warmth, and so the big arcaded building between Sliska and Sienna streets, the orphanage's second address since being moved to the ghetto, had become their home in October, shortly after their father's death.

Heavy steps came quickly, and the door was answered without delay. The big, much-lined face that appeared on the other side expressed both relief and irritation.

"Michal, the curfew began thirty minutes ago. If this goes on, you will not be allowed out on your own—it is an abuse of privilege."

"I'm sorry, Mrs. Stefa. . . ." Misha leaned back against the heavy door, which Mrs. Stefa had shut quickly behind him. She began putting up the security chains, then stopped and looked at him intently.

"Michal, child, whatever has happened?" He shook his head, without a word, and in a second the tall, plump, motherly woman, her annoyance melted, enveloped him in a bearlike hug. He accepted the comfort gratefully, though tears still refused to come. Very quickly he regained the new composure he'd found out there in Zelazna Street.

Disentangling himself, with his hands resting on her large forearms, he recounted simply the thing he had witnessed. At the end the only comment she made was, "Child, your eyes are like scorched holes in a blanket. There's still some soup in the kitchen—go and take some. Then get upstairs for some sleep."

Misha turned to walk into the kitchen, but didn't notice the small, slight, bald-headed figure coming down the stairs. The Doctor and Mrs. Stefa followed and watched as Misha peered into one of the huge tureens half-full of watery cabbage soup, then ladled a little into a dish. He studied the isolated vegetable shreds and then, with the hooked handle of the ladle, carefully removed three or four from his bowl and stirred them back into the broth. The two adults exchanged glances and sat down at the table. Misha, suddenly aware of their presence, looked from one to the other.

"Take some bread, child," the big woman almost barked. She got up and cut some of the gray, claylike substance that passed in those days for bread. Carefully she spread a layer of her clear beetroot marmalade on it, then stood back as if to admire her handiwork.

"But I've had some already today." Misha's protest was genuine enough, but lacked force. He looked to the Doctor for approval, who nodded and smiled.

"Go ahead, Misha." The sound of wild crying rang out. "That's little Monius—his temperature is right up again tonight." The Doctor shook his head in anxiety, the small furrows between his eyes meeting the bridge of his nose.

"I'll go. You stay." Mrs. Stefa bustled out, not waiting for argument.

"Michal, what happened tonight?" The old Doctor pronounced his name carefully, the hard *l* distinct.

"They've shot the Bergsons." Misha wondered if he ought perhaps to stop eating to break this somber news, but he was a slave to the craving in his stomach. He watched the small, red-bearded man who had become his family's savior; he noticed the deep furrows at the side of his eyes and thought how much more tired and ill he looked even compared with when he and his little sisters had come to live in the Orphans' Home. The thing in the well of his stomach stirred: Nothing must happen to the Doctor, for wasn't he the one rock capable of withstanding all the waves of fate?

The Doctor met his gaze and frowned questioningly. "The Bergsons?"

"You know, the baker in Zelazna Street. And his son. They were neighbors of ours—before."

"Oh, of course. How silly of me. They sent us fifty cakes at the last Passover, and I hadn't even asked for them. That wasn't the first time, either." He shook his head, just taking in what had happened. "Them, too. Them, too. Nice people."

The tears that murder, fear, and fury had failed to summon now welled into Misha's eyes. He made as if to take another spoonful of broth, but found the dish was already empty. Salt water dripped onto the spoon. The old Doctor leaned over, putting his hand on the boy's.

"Poor Misha," he whispered, now using his pet family name. "Child, like so many, without a childhood." He got up and began to pace the kitchen.

"Mister Doctor, *how* much longer will it go on?" Misha looked up at him earnestly, expecting an answer, yet knowing there was none.

There was a silence as Doctor Korczak idly picked up a ladle and stirred the tureen of cooling broth. "Misha, I do have faith that one day things will be better, but"—and he paused, not sure how much to say to this thin, anxious boy who always tried so hard to be brave—"but before they do, I fear they are going to get much worse."

The Doctor normally never talked in such a way to his children. Misha knew that the prophecy, as menacing as it was vague, was a sort of confidence, a mark of respect for his new-found maturity. Quietly, and with self-conscious dignity, he acknowledged as much: "Whatever happens, I hope I shall be worthy of your example."

One of the smaller children cried out at that moment, and without a word and with no more than the merest pressure of his hand on Misha's shoulder, the Doctor left the room.

CHAPTER 2

MISHA WENT UP TO the main dormitory on the first floor. It was actually a huge hall, in happier times used for dancing and still decorated with numerous pillars and mirrors. In the daytime it was used as a school and dining room, and then, thanks to Mrs. Stefa's ingenuity with old blankets and potato sacks, was transformed by the middle of the evening into a dormitory providing just a little privacy for each child. Misha made his way quietly to the end of one row of mattresses, just by the stairs leading up to the next floor. He peered over the makeshift partition: Yes, Rachel was still awake. She started up when she saw him, unashamedly pleased.

"*Misha*, I was *worried*," she exclaimed in her characteristically emphatic way.

"I'm sorry. I got a bit held up on the way back. Nothing to worry about."

"How's Mother?" Rachel's dark eyes watched him intently, frightened and hopeful at once.

"The same, Rachel. No better—but no worse, either." Rachel studied him, decided he was being frank, and then nodded, relieved. The times gave grim new meaning to the old cliché that "where there's life, there's hope."

"I *wish* I could go with you every time."

"I know. But Mister Doctor is right. It's safer for you to go with him, and, anyway, this way it gives Mother something special to look forward to."

Rachel nodded again, but doubtfully.

"Did you get a story tonight, Rachel?"

"No, Hanne had an asthma attack, and Sabina and Mister Doctor were just too busy. So many of the children are ill, Misha—last night I could hardly sleep for all the coughing."

"Shall I read to you now, quietly?"

Rachel looked delighted. *"Please."* He went around and sat on the end of her straw mattress. From under her pillow she produced one of her two well-worn storybooks and opened it at *The Snowstorm.*

"This one! Again!"

"Of course."

She sat up eagerly, cross-legged and hunched. Misha registered her enthusiasm, but also the hollow cheeks, the sallow complexion that had once glowed a healthy olive, and the yellowish tinge in the once clear whites of her eyes. He tried to read in a whisper, but before long his gruff adolescent voice had attracted more attention; two faces appeared over the sack partitioning, and then Hannah, Genia, and Romcia also arrived at the foot of the mattress. Misha gave them a shy smile and carried on reading, aware that he was probably providing these little girls with the highlight of their day. If he had imagined this scene a year ago, Misha would have blushed down to his toenails with embarrassment, but now he was only too pleased to see the rapt attention on their faces, and the embarrassment he did feel somehow had no sting.

The girls, though, were not yet beyond coyness and, if Misha had looked up between paragraphs, he might have caught Genia and Hannah nudging each other and giggling. Rachel hugged her knees and smiled, privately, into her lap; she knew her brother was a favorite in the home, and it made her feel proud and important. As he finished, five-year-old Romcia pleaded with him, using her huge blue eyes, to read them *her* favorite. Misha, now really rather bored but reluctant to disappoint his eager audience, was relieved when an adult voice intervened firmly:

"No, girls, it's time to try and sleep." Roza, one of the helpers and Romcia's mother, suddenly appeared. She smiled down at Misha in her friendly way.

"You go to bed, too, Michal. Thank him, all of you," she said, smoothing Romcia's not-over clean blond hair that in the daytime she wore in plaits like her mother's. Soap was scarce, and recently there had been more trouble with the water supply, which had been disconnected for several days. Mister Doctor had stalked off angrily one morning "to see someone about it," and a couple of hours after his return the taps had been running again. But the hairwashing rotation had been thrown off, among other things, and for the rest of that day the Doctor had seemed morose and more shut into himself than usual. Misha guessed he had had to use scarce orphanage supplies to bribe someone on the ghetto Water Board, and he knew he was right when he overheard Mrs. Stefa say to Roza. "Take this water business and those scoundrels at the Board. If only the poor man could rant and rave a bit like I do when things get too much. But he hates to say one cruel word, so he turns it all in on himself. What he suffers only God alone knows, if He can get it out of him."

Misha was surprised to find his own dormitory on the top floor already quiet and in darkness. He settled himself down under his two blankets before realizing that he hadn't looked in on baby Elena. With the few other very young children, she slept on the ground floor in the outer office, next to Mrs. Stefa's improvised office-bedroom. He frowned in the darkness; he shouldn't have forgotten to do that—that was hardly following the Doctor's example.

"Misha, any luck?" Viktor's eager voice hissed from the next mattress. Misha was irritated at having to admit he'd returned empty-handed.

"Not a sausage—literally."

"Nothing! What happened?"

"No idea. The brick hadn't even been moved. Maybe they forgot, or maybe they just had nothing to bring."

"Nothing! Nothing!" Viktor spat coarsely. "No one on the other side knows about *nothing*."

"Maybe I'll have better luck next time. Sorry. G'night."

"You'd better!" Misha smiled to himself, recognizing Viktor's bravado.

Before closing his eyes, he patted the little package under his pillow: The comforting bulge was still there. In a way he was quite glad that his contact hadn't turned up and that he hadn't been able to exchange the two leather belts as planned. His mother had money for her immediate needs, and the very feel of the belts—his father's own craftsmanship—gave him a sense of reassurance. Provided he could find another outlet, and that shouldn't be difficult, they guaranteed food for his mother for at least another couple of weeks—and a couple of weeks was a future. And he had the wallets and silver cufflinks, too.

CHAPTER 3

W HEN MISHA'S FAMILY HAD arrived in the ghetto in October 1940, they had been fortunate enough to find quite decent accommodations, a relatively large, drafty flat in a building near the corner of Orla and Leszno streets, close to the Christian church that stood like a sentry beside its patch of precious green yard. For when the Nazis had built their three meters wall sealing the Jewish ghetto off from the rest of Warsaw, they had seen to it that all the capital's lovely parks remained outside the ghetto confines. The result was that a generation of small children were growing up for whom green and growing things belonged not to the everyday world around them but to the world of picture books and fairy stories; for their older brothers and sisters they belonged to the wistful world of memory. Doctor Korczak had brought with him from the former Orphans' Home in Krochmalna Street a supply of his beloved geraniums, which he propagated and nurtured with characteristic care. The plants had not only cheered up the new building, but also helped him give the children lessons in elementary botany. He had given Rachel two cuttings, which she was tending with great anxiety as a present for their mother's birthday in June.

But on this April Sabbath their mother's drab bed-sitting room was decorated only by Rachel's drawings. Mrs. Edelman had withdrawn into one room after her husband's death and the children's departure, so as to free the other two rooms for one of the refugee families who had been herded into the ghetto from outside Warsaw, trebling the imprisoned population. The furniture in this room was all that was left of the Edelmans' formerly comfortable existence: the big bed, minus its brass headboard, the mahogany sideboard, and the table and chairs. All smaller items, even the footstool his grandmother had once embroidered, had long ago been exchanged for food or fuel. The sideboard would probably have met with the same fate had it not been too cumbersome for Misha to handle, though it was amazing what sort of things did make their way through the wall at certain points. This morning Misha eyed the four upright chairs thoughtfully. Then he felt his mother's gaze upon him and was embarrassed; after all, they still needed those chairs when they met together as a family.

He stirred the watery broth over what passed for a coal-dust fire. Mrs. Edelman was propped up against several pillows, smiling at her son.

"I feel better today, Misha. I thought perhaps I'd get up for a while."

He looked up eagerly, a flash of hope lighting his thin, white face.

"That's *good*. I've put something special in here today, too, so you can have it sitting up at the table." Then, even brighter at the afterthought: "Rachel will be pleased if you're up when she gets here."

"I'm so looking forward to seeing her. And Eli, too."

"Of course." Misha poked at the glowing coal dust, hiding his face. There was a busy silence. Then Mrs. Edelman said gently, "Misha, please come here."

Misha dropped the poker and went immediately to her bedside. In another place, another time, with all the strength and spirit he had at his command, he might have been less amenable, less desperate to please. As it was, he treated each hour with his mother as if it were the last. He stood looking down at her, his forehead puckered, his hands hanging heavy and awkward at his sides. She touched one with one of her own, in which the veins protruded, knotted and blue.

"Misha, I know it's been hard for you to accept Elena. I know she doesn't belong to our happier times, but remember, darling, she does belong to *us*. To Daddy, too." There was a pause.

Someone dropped something heavy on the other side of the thin partition wall, and voices were raised in anger.

"Mother," he said eventually, "it's not that I don't accept Elena. I do—really. Some of the time I think I even love her. But I just seem to . . . well, forget about her at times. It sounds dreadful, I know, but she just seems sort of—tacked on. Don't be sad. I'm sure it won't feel like that as she gets older."

His mother looked at him affectionately.

"I'm not sad. You're a good boy. You should be able to hate both your little sisters and think of them as a nuisance without feeling guilty about it. That's just another thing you've been denied." She held on to his hand; he would have liked to jerk it away and run out of the room, but he dared do nothing, not the slightest thing, that might hurt this frail, vulnerable woman. Yet he felt that her understanding was only partial; her loving dismissal of what had seemed to him a momentous confession was somehow unsatisfactory. The point was, he didn't want to hate *both* his sisters; Rachel was all right, Rachel was bright, Rachel was lively, Rachel was, despite the pale, now quite sickly, look about her, a tough little creature who commanded a sort of respect. Perhaps Elena would be like that one day, but all she was good for at the moment, he reflected bitterly, was to remind him of his dead father, so striking was the resemblance in her eyes and in the shape of her little face.

"Shall I help you up now?" he asked, glad to be able to change the subject. When she was settled at the table, he put the broth in front of her with a triumphant "There!"

"Michal! Carrots, potatoes, and cabbage. A feast!" She laughed and clapped her hands with delight, though not with much sound. They smiled at each other, sharing a moment of joy. For a second Misha had a vision of his tenth, or perhaps his eleventh birthday, when the table at home had, for all the shortages of the war, seemed laden with cakes and fruit. The pleasure he'd felt at the unusual sight of that table was as nothing compared with this.

"Come on, share this with me."

"No, no, no, mine'll come later." Misha backed away, uncertain how much insistence he'd be able to withstand.

At that moment there was a flurry of knocks at the door, and Rachel burst in, followed closely by the Doctor, carrying eighteen-month-old Elena.

"*Mother!*" cried Rachel, running up to her eagerly, then pausing, suddenly remembering instructions not to be too boisterous, before kissing her gently on the cheek. She dropped a rather crumpled piece of paper on the table beside the dish of soup, her weekly offering of a color drawing. Quite a sizable art collection was accumulating in the room, with pictures propped up wherever there was a place to prop them—glue, of course, being virtually unobtainable.

"We're on to the backs of flour sacks now," smiled Mister Doctor, shaking his head at the fragment of paper. "But the decorations are improving steadily. One of the stars of Sabina's art class, aren't you, Rachel?"

"They're *lovely*. Some of my most precious possessions." And Mrs. Edelman kissed her elder daughter. Then she held out her arms toward the whimpering toddler, and her loose sleeves fell back, betraying the thinness of her arms.

"Mister Doctor"—for even Mrs. Edelman called him that now—"the potatoes and carrots! You're so kind. But I feel I'm robbing you and . . ."

"I only send them when we can spare them—I've told you that before. Two rather rude letters to the Jewish Supply Authority produced two hundred kilos of potatoes for the children the other day, so Misha and I thought we could divert one or two in your direction." The two adults exchanged glances: They both knew there was a very good reason why the Doctor tried, whenever he could, to help Misha provide for his near-helpless mother.

Presently Misha and Rachel were sent off to the next-door flat with Elena, where there lived a family of refugees from the south. "Rachel, those little girls from next door come in to see me nearly every day asking when you'll be here next. They think the world of you, and they do love making a fuss of Eli."

When they'd gone, the Doctor sat down at the table opposite Mrs. Edelman. He spoke in a low voice, as if afraid of being overheard.

"The news from the east is bad, Lili, very bad. I don't want to cause you extra worry, but I really fear now for the children. And the consequences of being caught smuggling are now— well, worse than they've been all along. I don't have the same control over Misha as I do over the younger ones—and I don't forbid him to smuggle, because . . ."

The Doctor took off his glasses as he often did when looking for the right words. He was a naturally shy man who found it far easier to commit words to paper or to talk to children than to other adults. He struggled now to express himself in a way that would not be hurtful.

Lili Edelman rescued him: "I know. He smuggles for me; it's Misha who is keeping me alive. The greatest torment of many of us ghetto mothers is knowing that our sons and daughters are risking their lives for us every day. There are three others like me in this building alone. But, Mister Doctor, I don't think I can stop him—and if I could, where would that leave him?"

The Doctor kept his gaze fixed on the table, scratching at it with his thumbnail.

"No, you can't stop him," he said slowly. "But neither can I. And that's really what I wanted to be clear between us. You relinquished him to my care in the spirit of love; it's in the same spirit that I deny him the protection he needs. Such a strange situation." And he shook his head sadly.

"I know that. Of course I know that." She would have liked to put out her hand and touch his, but there was something about the Doctor that seemed to welcome only the physical touch of children. "But don't forget how much you *have* given them, will you? Not just Misha and Rachel and Eli, but all of them. Never ever forget that, Janusz." She suddenly recognized the need for comfort and strength in this wasting, aging man who had still to be the comfort and strength of so many.

There was a brief silence, neither of them knowing quite how to continue. Then Lili Edelman asked tremulously, "And the news from Chelmno? Do you think it's true what they're saying, that there's a big camp there set up just to murder Jews?"

"Well, the reports of the escaped gravediggers aren't exactly encouraging. Last month Chelmno, this month the rounding up of Jews in Lublin. I'm afraid there can be little doubt as to what's intended for us. But, Lili, I must ask you quickly before the children come back. Is there *anyone* left they could possibly go to on the other side?"

"No, there's no one. Last year Jan's cousin and her family were still in Warsaw, but as you know Misha and Rachel absolutely refused to leave us. You remember—it was hard enough to persuade them to come to you."

"Yes, I remember." He understood the defensive note in her voice. But he had to carry on: "And *your* cousins? No longer here?"

"No. He thought his blue eyes and blond hair made him safe, but he was wrong. He may not have been counted a Jew, but he was good Polish slave labor to *them*. They've carted him off to the Reich—to work in one of their armament factories, most likely. Anna took the children to her people in the south—they have a farm down there. We kept in touch by phone till the lines were cut last summer." Then, as an afterthought, "I wrote to them when Jan died, but I've heard nothing, so maybe something's happened to them, too." She leaned back, tired after her unusually long speech. She coughed a little, but the Doctor felt he had to persist.

"And there's no one else?"

"No one. And no money, either. I know the sort of sums that are changing hands for taking in our children over there. I've got nothing remotely like that. A few pieces of Jan's leatherwork and a thousand zloty for you, for—for—well, for whatever. But that's all that's left now." She shook her head, and there was a note of panic in her voice.

"I might, you see, be able to help. I still have a lot of contacts on the other side . . . if that's what you would like."

"But I've told you. I've no *money*."

"I may be able to arrange something, all the same. You must understand that I can't make any promises, but if it's what you want, I will try."

"Want," she repeated dully, and this time a fit of coughing overcame her. The spasms that shook her body came as an odd sort of relief; her mind was jerked away from whether or not she "wanted" to part forever with one or all of her children in order to give them no more than a dubious advantage in the fight for survival.

"Has it *really* come to this?" she said eventually, her voice hoarse with coughing, or dread, or both. "Janusz, this is Europe, this is the twentieth century, not the dark ages or the jungle. *Surely* they can't mean to kill us *all*?"

The Doctor rubbed his bald head; he had been up writing for much of the night before and had then risen at six. He ached with exhaustion in all his limbs, and he had to fight down real physical nausea at the thought of two more of those dreadful begging calls still to be made that day. The Home was running short of flour, and he had heard that he might even be able to get hold of some eggs at the brush factory on Gesia Street. The ghetto "shops" and "factories," which produced goods for and under the supervision of the Nazis, enjoyed better rations and were often fruitful hunting grounds for supplies.

He would have liked to comfort her with some sort of assurance, but his powers of pretense—never very great—had been severely overtaxed by his two hundred young charges, who depended on him for at least some belief in a future. The specter of what was to come loomed up out of his weary silence, and Mrs. Edelman grasped the edges of the table in an attempt to balance the dark ball of fear hanging heavy within her.

At that moment the door opened and Rachel came in almost at a run.

"Mother, *look* what we've got for you!" The refugees next door were not the quietest of neighbors, but they were warmhearted and kind. They had a relative who worked in the synthetic honey shop and they'd given Rachel a little jar of the bright, gloriously sweet stuff to present to her mother.

Doctor Korczak took advantage of the interruption.

"I must go now. I'll try and be back for the girls in under two hours." To Misha, who was still on the landing politely trying to get away from talkative Mrs. Stein, he said firmly, "I'd be grateful for your help in taking them back to the Orphans' Home." Misha understood only too well the look that passed between the two grown-ups, and he felt cross and frustrated. He pressed the leather belt in the frayed lining of his jacket with disappointment and carried Elena into his mother's room with less than his customary gentleness.

CHAPTER 4

THAT NIGHT MISHA NO longer felt reassured as he pressed the little bundle of leather goods hidden in his mattress. The smuggling arrangement he had made clearly couldn't be relied on anymore, if he stopped to think about it; it was the Doctor who hadn't given him a chance to go back to the cemetery wall that afternoon, it was true, but the last three journeys across the ghetto had been fruitless. Was it possible that Felek or his brother had been arrested? He hoped not; they'd been good customers of his father in the old days. Perhaps they thought the risk had become just too great. In any case, the exchange point in the cemetery was too faraway from Sienna Street—as far again as his mother's room from the Orphans' Home—and more and more he hated walking through the ghetto streets. They were so crowded and noisy and dirty, and twice now he had stumbled over corpses lying in doorways, one of which hadn't even been covered with newspaper. He shuddered as he remembered the open, sightless eyes. He always came back tired and cross and, oh, so *hungry*. But the cemetery's one big advantage was that it had been relatively safe, since there were plenty of carts and gravestones to hide behind, should a patrol appear. There was no obvious place more nearby that offered as much cover. Anyway, first things first: Before he could even think of a new exchange point, he had to establish a new contact. And that, of course, meant crossing over to the other side. Not a pleasant prospect. Misha turned over yet again on the lumpy straw mattress encased in newspaper, which was all that was left to the children since the Nazis had confiscated all the decent bedding. The penalty for being caught on the other side was certain death—he might be shot straightaway, if he were searched and could produce no papers; or he might be brought back into the ghetto and made into an example. He remembered the "show" executions of the previous November and drew the thin blankets more closely around him. But perhaps he was being too gloomy. After all, he'd managed to get across by the Twarda Street gate several times before.

Not since last October though, said the voice of gloom inside him again. And that time he'd had to sacrifice half his hard-won prize of garden pears because Joseph had wanted his reward for looking the other way. Would Joseph still be at that gate? It was possible. He wasn't really to be trusted, of course, but he was probably as near to a decent chap as a Jewish policeman could be. Eventually, his decision half-made, Misha dozed off into a shallow, unrefreshing sleep. He dreamed that he was caught trying to escape through the ghetto gates and was shot, but in agonizingly slow motion. He woke once or twice to a sense of intense relief to find himself still alive; but each time he gave way again to sleep, the same dreams resumed. Adziu, a boy with an outstandingly tragic past even by the Orphans' Home standards, slept with a bayonet under his mattress at the far end of the dormitory. In Misha's dream he rose up from a manhole, covered in filth, grinning and beckoning as Misha sank slowly to the ground. Adziu had regularly negotiated the sewers in the service of one of the ghetto's really big-time smugglers before Mister Doctor had come upon him and "kidnapped" him for the Orphans' Home. When Misha woke finally next morning, he did wonder if the dream had been some sort of message telling him to take the sewer route to the Aryan side; but with his air-raid-inspired terror of being buried alive, this was quite, quite unthinkable.

It was not difficult to slip away next morning on the little reconnaissance mission he had planned. It was the day the Doctor had arranged for some of the older children to have religious education classes with Rabbi Gutman in Sliska Street; Misha was actually sorry to miss the weekly class because the Rabbi was a nice old man with a store of good anecdotes and stories that he delighted in sharing with his young audience. But he was vague and his sight was failing and he never really succeeded in getting to know the children as individuals, so Misha was confident that his absence would not be noticed.

Halfway down Sienna Street, Misha heard a breathless, "Wait for me, for goodness' sake." He turned around to see Viktor running laboriously after him, flushed and puffed.

"But . . ."

"Please, Misha, please let me come, too." Misha wasn't sure whether to be pleased or irritated; he was quite glad of the company in one way but at the same time had a suspicion he'd be quicker and quieter, and therefore safer, on his own. But he took pity on Viktor's anxious face:

"Come on, then, but hurry up. Rabbi Gutman's going to have a small class today!"

About fifty meters from the Twarda Street gate they stopped in a corner doorway and watched. There were two Nazis and two Jewish policemen on guard; Misha didn't recognize any of them. The gate was quiet, though a few groups of ragged children were standing around, probably waiting for the right moment to try to slip through to the other side. Misha noticed that both Jewish policemen seemed to be getting on well with the two Nazis, and he felt a surge of hate as he remembered his father talking bitterly of Jewish traitors. His father had felt this keenly, for his own brother, Misha's uncle, had become a policeman and had, to his family's shame, joined with enthusiasm in the rounding up of Jewish men and women to be sent to the labor camps in Hitler's Germany. Misha now looked at these policemen's starred caps and arm bands, at their rubber clubs and high shiny boots, and he remembered Mr. Bergson and his son Marek lying crumpled and dead, as other similar boots marched away.

The two SS guards began to play a game with two of the children—boys, and probably no more than seven or eight years old, though size was often misleading in those hungry days. The game featured two shiny apples as balls, and the two little boys as piggies-in-the-middle. As Misha watched them reach up with their emaciated arms, each time putting all their energy into little ecstasies of hope unthwarted by continual failure, he was moved again to rage. But it was an impotent, useless rage, for he could do nothing to help them. He couldn't even move, except deeper into the shadow of the wall.

Suddenly the guards began shouting. The callous game ended abruptly and the little "opponents" were chased away with rifle butts, one of the Jewish policemen joining in. There were answering shouts from beyond the three-meter-high gates, and then, as they were swung open, a truckload of workers came into view—people who had been laboring outside the ghetto on the night shift. Misha had long ago sold the watch his parents had given him for his eleventh birthday—it had fetched a loaf of black bread, and a wonderfully welcome kilo of plums—but a clock that still worked on one of the buildings across the road told him that it was almost nine o'clock. That was important to remember. He narrowed his eyes and watched carefully as the truckload of workers was counted and inspected. One or two people were ordered down, and they stood wearily while they were searched for smuggled food. All the orders and questions were shouted in harsh monosyllables: Misha realized, as he watched and listened, that he'd never heard a Nazi speak in a normal voice. The one who had laughed loudest during the piggy-in-the-middle game was now shouting the loudest. Misha saw him rip a hearing aid away from a white-haired old man and crush it under his boot. "You won't need this, Grandpa," he trumpeted in German. "We'll shout loud enough for you to hear." Misha watched as the old man was pushed back into the truck and how, as it started up again and lurched toward the unloading point, his gaze remained fixed on the spot on the ground where his little device lay squashed and useless.

Misha and Viktor had seen enough. While the guards were preoccupied with shutting the gate and logging the truck's return, they slipped quietly away down the street and were soon mingling with the crowd. Before they were out of earshot of the gate, though, they heard a shriek that made them start with alarm; but when they looked back, it was only the game of piggy-in-the-middle starting again.

Back in Sienna Street they were greeted with cries of delight as they slipped through the courtyard and into the house via the kitchen.

"*Misha*, come and help. *Look* what we've got. Come on. Where have you *been*?" Misha had no time for fibs—Rachel was pressing a knife and a turnip into his willing hands and showing him the sacks of carrots, beets, and turnips that had just arrived as a gift for the Orphans' Home from one of the factories.

"Look at them all. Mrs. Stefa says we can have potato pancakes tonight and turnip soup. There are eggs, too. Real ones—not powdered." Rachel turned back to the sink, her knife skimming almost lovingly over the potato in her left hand. Viktor, meanwhile, had been drafted into helping at the other sink by two of the other girls on kitchen duty, who laughed with glee at his clumsy efforts.

Rachel continued to work busily for a few minutes, then suddenly remembered something. She put down her knife and turned to Misha with serious eyes. "Where were you earlier? I came up to see you after breakfast . . ."

"You know Rabbi Gutman's classes are on Thursdays."

"Misha, don't lie to me. I know very well they were cancelled today—Musik and the others were told not to go because the Rabbi is ill. But I'd have known you were lying, anyway—it's written all over your face."

Misha grinned and looked sheepish. "Caught red-handed, I suppose." They looked at each other and laughed a little. Then Rachel went on: "Come on, tell me. Have you been back to that graveyard? You *know* what Mother has said about that." She reached into the sack for another potato and, though she spoke reproachfully, when she straightened up and looked at him again, there was more pride than disapproval in her face.

Misha was aware that the group at the other sink had become momentarily quiet.

"I can't tell you now, but I will later. I may need your help, anyway." He couldn't imagine how he might need her help but knew that a touch of conspiracy would please her, and he was indeed rewarded with a smile and a wink.

"I think I'll stop now," she said presently. She brushed the peelings into a large pan, covered them with cold water, and set them aside by the range. Misha noticed how she had to hold the pan handle with both arms to keep it steady.

"You should have let me do that."

"I'm not fading away *yet*." But she did look tired suddenly, and it was no surprise when she said, "I think I'll go up and write in my diary before lessons."

She often felt the need for short rests during the day—what energy her undernourished body afforded her, she used up quickly and without thought of conservation. Misha made a face, but without letting Rachel see. Privately he thought diaries were a bit silly, even though the Doctor encouraged all the older children to keep them.

When she'd gone, Misha sat down at the large wooden table and watched the others working; their chatter had now subsided.

"One, two, three," Genia counted each potato lovingly, until she reached ten. "There, we must stop now. Mrs. Stefa said not to do more than ten per helper." She looked around for a pan. "Misha, why are you looking so sad?"

Misha looked up at his sister's friend; she was a large-boned, rather plain girl, but with kind blue eyes and a friendly word for everyone—especially for Misha. There was, however, something about her that seemed to invite rebuff, and Misha had more than once heard Musik and Adziu say unkind, sarcastic things to her. Now, just for a moment, he, too, felt tempted to tell her to mind her own business, but he checked himself in time. After all, there was no reason to snub her—she meant so well, and like everyone else at the Orphans' Home, Genia had had her fair share of personal tragedy. But there was an unwritten rule in the orphanage that you put a brave face on your sadness, for your own sake as well as for everyone else's.

"Not really sad, Genia—just thoughtful."

"Good. Coming to history later?"

"Just try and keep me away!"

"For all the wrong reasons, I suppose." Genia dried her hands briskly, making them red. One of the helpers, lovely dark-eyed Nacia, who had only just embarked on her teaching career when war broke out, gave the older children lessons in Polish history twice a week, and these lessons, held in the office, were always particularly well attended by the teenage boys.

When Genia left the room, Viktor, who had been leaning silently against the sink studying his worn-out shoes, sat down at the table opposite Misha. Viktor was unappealing to look at, with his white pimply complexion and sandy hair. Misha's feelings toward him alternated between irritation and protectiveness when the other boys teased him, and as a result he had earned Viktor's unswerving devotion.

"I've been thinking," he announced, taking off his glasses and wiping them with a frayed cuff.

"I wouldn't do too much of that if I were you—uses up valuable energy. Well?"

"That Jewish policeman, the one who helped chase the little boys away when the night shift came back—I know him."

"So?"

"Well, he may be able to help us get over to the other side." Misha uttered a swearword in German: It had so much more venom in that language.

"You must be out of your tiny mind!" he went on. "You saw the way he treated those little kids. What makes you think he'll be so different with us?"

Viktor put on a typical Viktor expression, hurt and bewildered. But he persevered. "I'm not so sure," he said slowly. "You see, we knew his family quite well before. His mother's a nice lady. When my ma died, she used to come around quite often with things she'd cooked." Misha had hardly ever heard Viktor mention his mother directly; as he did so now, he looked Misha straight in the eye, almost as if to challenge him.

"All right, so even Jewish policemen occasionally have nice mothers. But in this case it obviously hasn't rubbed off on the son." Misha was privately quite pleased with that reply.

"Okay. You're good with words and cleverer than me—I know that. But it's easy to make fun of things. I'm going to give it a try anyway. You can stay behind if you like." Misha looked up, surprised at Viktor's unusual determination.

"It's crazy. Absolutely crazy. Wait a day or two to see if Joseph comes back on duty at Twarda."

"Everything we do in this ghetto is crazy, if you mean dangerous. I don't see what's so different about this. Or are you losing your nerve?"

Fortunately for Viktor, who was not at all comfortable in this defiant role, Mrs. Stefa came bustling in at that moment, gripping two eight-year-old boys by the arm. She was scolding them loudly for fighting; one already had a distinctly swollen eye.

"Find the disinfectant for me, Misha, there's a good boy," she cried, and Viktor took the opportunity to slip quietly away.

CHAPTER 5

DURING THE HISTORY LESSON, Misha studiously avoided looking at Viktor. He knew, despite the way he had mocked Viktor's idea, that a decision would have to be made—and soon. He would have liked to put off the moment, but his mind kept returning to it as if it had a will of its own. Viktor was right: Almost everything they did in that ghetto, outside the Orphans' Home, and certainly anything to do with smuggling, *was* dangerous—deadly dangerous. Money had to be obtained, and the graveyard source had almost certainly dried up. And one gate guard was probably as callous as another, so why was he hesitating? Had he lost his nerve? Was it the way that SS bully had crushed the old man's hearing aid? Or the tantalizingly cruel way he had thrown the apples only just beyond the little boys' reach? But perhaps, after all, the old man had been lucky; another guard, another mood, and the gray head might have been battered instead of the ear gadget.

"What do *you* think, Misha?" Nacia asked suddenly. Misha started and blushed; he hadn't been listening to one word of the lesson, though normally he was fascinated by accounts of battles raging over the Polish plains. But Nacia was more apologetic than her pupil: "I'm sorry—don't worry, Misha. I'll ask . . . let's see, Maria." Nacia always made a point of stressing that her lessons were voluntary and the last thing she would have wanted to do was embarrass any of the children in front of the others. Misha looked at her approvingly; how did she manage to keep her dark hair so sleek and shiny, he wondered, when everyone else's was dull or greasy through lack of water or soap.

After lunch—potato soup in three sittings, starting with the youngest children—Misha went up to his room on the third floor. The one advantage of sleeping at the top of the house, despite the icy temperatures in winter, was the relative privacy afforded during the daytime. At least the older boys didn't have to move their mattresses to make way for meals and lessons. Each boy had improvised some sort of bedside table of packing cases or boxes; Pieter Goldszmidt, a carpenter by trade, came once a week to give them carpentry lessons, and one or two of the boys had made quite reasonable pieces of furniture out of scraps of wood and chipboard. They wondered, sometimes, about these pieces of wood, but it didn't do to ask too many questions.

Misha's talents, however, did not lie in a practical direction. He could draw quite well and, because he had always enjoyed reading and writing, he was on the editorial committee of the weekly orphanage gazette. His particular editorial responsibility was to sift through the entries to the essay competition, which was always popular—too popular, he sometimes thought, as he plowed through the umpteenth entry on "My Favorite Meal" or "What I Want To Be When I Grow Up" on their scrappy bits of paper—to compile a short list. It was often difficult for him to be absolutely fair and impartial, particularly since Rachel was undoubtedly the most competent writer in her age group and the most original.

Today he sighed as he settled down on his mattress, his back against the wall, to read through the week's entries. He was tired and would have liked to doze, but at the same time felt restless and more than usually churned up in the pit of his stomach. He was frowning at Maria's third repetition of the same adjective in one sentence when the door slowly opened to reveal Viktor. He stood there hesitantly, his hands hanging limp by his sides, and said shyly, "Misha, I'm sorry for what I said. You've got more guts than I'll ever have. I just wanted—oh, I don't know, the chance to . . ." He took off his glasses, unsure how far to commit himself.

"Oh, for goodness' sake, forget it. Come and give me a hand with these, will you? Don't forget—put the corrections at the bottom. Mister Doctor says it's discouraging to see words crossed out."

Viktor approached eagerly, unable to disguise his relief. He took some of the essays on their scraps of assorted paper and settled himself on his own mattress.

There followed quite a long silence before Misha said casually, without taking his eyes off the particularly messy contribution in front of him, "You're right, actually. There is no ideal place and Twarda Street's probably as good as any, despite everything we saw. Shall we go for it tomorrow?"

Viktor gave a low whistle. "*Great*. Thanks, Mish."

"No need to thank me. Common sense, really. The trouble *is*, of course, that if we have to slip over with a work shift, we'll have to wait for them to come back, so we're bound to be missed here."

"Well, surely Rachel can say you've gone to see your mother—and taken me with you," Viktor suggested promptly. He'd worked that one out already.

"Mister Doctor knows I usually go to see Mother in the afternoons. He'll know what's up—he knows very well how I've managed to keep Mother going." There was a note of pride in his voice. Then, "I *wonder* what happened to Felek and his brother. They were always so reliable." There was another silence while their imaginations suggested all too many answers to the question.

"Anyway," Misha went on decisively, "I don't want Rachel brought in on this. No, we'll just have to go—and take the consequences later. Mister Doctor has to go out so much at the moment and everyone else is so fantastically busy—you never know—we might just get away with it. Adziu seems to, all the time."

Stash and Stefan came in then, so no more could be said.

Stash was a good-natured boy but not the best person at keeping secrets. Though very diffident, he was talented with his hands and had made beautiful puppets for the orphanage puppet theater out of old bits of wood. He was in high spirits today. Doctor Korczak had just made special arrangements for him to spend two days a week with Pieter Goldszmidt, helping him in his workshop. In the old days one of the jobs the Doctor used to find most rewarding was discovering ways of developing his children's talents; before the war the boys had always been sent out to jobs or apprenticeships when they became fourteen. Nowadays the Doctor hated the idea of having to turn his precious charges loose in the ghetto jungle without the means of making a living, and he had been known to forget fourteenth birthdays.

"Who knows what I might be able to pick up," Stash was crowing. He paused. "If I'm good enough to stay . . ."

"All right for some," remarked Stefan who, grumpy as usual, ignored his friend's need for reassurance.

"Shut up, will you—some of us have work to do," commanded Misha pleasantly; without looking up he added, "Of course you'll be good enough, Stash."

The next morning was gray, damp, and windy, weather that oddly enough was quite welcome in the ghetto since it made less obvious the absence of trees and green spaces and even seemed to wash some of the grime and smell from the streets. Misha and Viktor walked down Sienna Street, keeping close to the houses as usual. Sienna Street, being on the edge of the ghetto and in one of its comparatively "smart" sections, was not as crowded or noisy as the more central streets, but there were always plenty of things going on all the same. This morning, though still not long after eight o'clock, they were accosted by two women, both trying to sell homemade wares at the junction with Sosnowa Street—some gray-looking biscuits in one case, and, in the other, some obviously secondhand arm bands bearing the yellow star of David, which it was compulsory for all Jews in the ghetto to wear on their right sleeves. Misha couldn't help wondering what had happened to the previous owners. The boys shook their heads and hurried on until they reached the doorway that had sheltered them the day before.

As they had hoped, the same two Jewish policemen were on duty. Viktor eyed his man carefully as he walked aimlessly up and down and then joined his colleague in the sentry booth. The other man was bending over, looking at something; he must have made some joke, probably crude, because a gust of hearty laughter could be heard from where the boys were standing nearly a hundred meters away. Right on schedule, just before nine o'clock, the truckload of night-shift workers arrived outside the gates. There were no SS guards in sight as yet this morning, but two of the blue Polish police were there, and it was they who opened the gates. Then it seemed as if all four policemen were suddenly shouting orders up at the weary passengers as soon as they rolled into sight, and one or two were ordered down to be searched. Misha scanned the truck for the old man who had lost his hearing aid, but he wasn't to be seen. Viktor's man did seem to be letting his colleague do most of the work and stood by watching the proceedings. Misha shut his eyes then; he had heard an unmistakable scrabbling in the wall of the house beside him that made him shudder, for he had always reacted to vermin as some people do to snakes. For some reason, and without warning, Viktor chose that precise moment for his great gamble, because when Misha opened his eyes again, Viktor had left his side and was walking boldly up to the tall man in the starred cap and arm bands. Misha now heard a squeaking behind the bricks in the doorway and more scurrying, and he felt distinctly sick. He saw the big policeman wheel around, saw him look down at Viktor and seem to listen to him; there was an everlasting pause while the thumping of Misha's own heart conducted another chorus of squeaks behind him; then a great theatrical roar—and Viktor was on his knees in a puddle on the cobblestones.

Misha did not stop to consider. The wrath he had felt the night the Bergsons were shot flared up inside him and sent him running to Viktor's side. Viktor was groping around desperately for his glasses, and the big thug with the star on his cap was yelling, "Clear off, you scum. We're not playing games today. Clear off—you, too." And he gave Misha a shove with his black boot.

"He can't clear off if he can't see. He has to find his glasses." Misha looked up at Viktor's assailant with hate-given calm.

"Hold your tongue and clear off." The giant of a man turned away, apparently no longer interested in such small fry. Misha bent down to help his friend, who had received a substantial blow to the side of his head and was still feeling dizzy. As he did so, he caught sight of the glasses, which had rolled a few feet toward the guards' booth. Without hesitation, but with something like a stone in his stomach, Misha walked toward the glasses, his eyes fixed on the spot where they lay. As he made to pick them up, a shiny black boot appeared and rested an inch or two above them. Misha looked up. One of the blue policemen was now grinning hideously down at him.

"Say please, Jewboy."

Misha paused, then straightened up, but not for one second did he stop looking the policeman in the eye. Eventually he heard himself say with icy precision, "Please, Mister Policeman, may I have the glasses back without which my friend is unable to see?"

"Rude little rascal," barked the young man, but he removed his boot from the glasses. Misha bent down quickly to retrieve them, but as he straightened up he felt a sharp, searing pain in his right thigh. The boot had had its game after all.

As if by some tacit agreement, the boys retreated from the

gate at a walk, not a run. But once out of sight around the corner in Sienna Street, they immediately broke into a trot. Or Viktor did, for Misha's leg was already painful and he had to drag it, cursing under his breath in violent and incorrect German. Viktor, as he adjusted his pace to Misha's, sadly assessed the damage to his glasses.

"Oh, well, only one crack. I suppose it could have been much worse. Just like the Doctor's now."

Misha put a hand out to his shoulder and panted. "Bad luck." His thigh glowed hot with pain, but he was aware of a different glow inside, for he knew he had behaved with courage, even recklessness.

"Mish, you were fantastic—just fantastic! But I think you may have managed—to—mess—the—whole—thing—up. I can't—keep going." Viktor stopped and bent down to touch his knee, troubled by a stitch as well as breathlessness.

"What on earth do you mean?" Misha demanded, at a standstill now, too. He was very taken aback.

"You see, just before he hit me, he told me under his breath to come back tomorrow when different guards'll be on duty. He said he . . . knew them better. That's all, but I assumed that meant he'd help us. I must say, it came as a bit of a shock when he yelled and lashed out." He gingerly put a hand to the side of his face.

"I hate to say 'I told you so.'"

"He was acting up for the sake of the other guards, Misha. I'm sure he was. The blues were taking it all in, and the SS won't have been far away. Mind where you're going, idiot!" This last was at a boy about his own age who bumped his leg with a little handcart as he hurried by.

"Your faith is touching. The others were far too busy swearing at the night shift to watch your friend."

"Okay, then, Mister Know-it-all. Why did he say, 'Come back tomorrow'?" Viktor's question was high-pitched, and tears welled up in his eyes. They had turned to face each other on the pavement. Gray people milled around them in the gray street, but no one took any interest; street confrontations were commonplace and this wasn't an exciting one.

Misha didn't know the answer, of course. He didn't know the answer to anything anymore. He just stood there and shrugged, suddenly feeling exhausted.

"Boys, what *is* the matter?" They were startled by the Doctor himself, carrying two rather awkward packages on his way back to the Orphans' Home. They were, in fact, almost there.

"What ever is happening?" Doctor Korczak looked from one to the other, his blue eyes behind the thick cracked glasses taking it all in. Misha and Viktor exchanged sheepish glances; it was not easy to lie to the Doctor, but neither of them wanted to tell him what they'd been up to—they knew it could only add to his worries.

"Bit of a fight really, that's all, Mister Doctor," stuttered Viktor.

"And I cracked his glasses," added Misha, looking every bit as guilty as if he had in fact done the damage himself.

"No, he didn't!" Viktor couldn't let that one pass. "He was brave, Mister Doctor, *really* brave. One of the Polish policemen—he was going to smash them with his boot—but Misha stood up to him—told him to give them to me—and—and he did." Tears were now rolling freely down Viktor's freckled cheeks.

"Come, help me with these now. Let's get home as soon as we can," said their guardian firmly. Misha, glad to hide his embarrassment, concentrated on helping with the more cumbersome of the two packages and began to walk sideways, a gait that only accentuated his newly acquired limp.

"Do you want to know what you're carrying?" The boys nodded eagerly. "Bits of wool and cloth for Sabina's sewing class!" Their faces fell. "And in Viktor's there are two 3-kilo hams!" Now neither of them had any difficulty in looking interested, and the Doctor smiled at them, sharing their pleasure. "That'll brighten up the broth for a few days, won't it? A pity it had to be ham—but what can we do?"

CHAPTER 6

LATER ON, WHEN MISHA had washed in an attempt to purge himself of the morning's ugly business and lain down on his mattress to flick wearily through the remaining essays, the Doctor came in search of him. He asked him to come down with him to his room. In fact, he shared what was rather meaninglessly called the "isolation room" with the sickest children, so as to be quickly available if needed. He gestured to Misha to sit in the one chair, while he leaned back against his desk.

"First, I want to look at that leg. And second, I'd like you to tell me what happened this morning."

Misha nodded and obediently rolled up his trouser leg; it was wide bottomed and slipped back easily to reveal a hard swelling above the knee, already quite discolored. The Doctor felt around the injury with practiced fingers.

"Nothing broken, but a nasty bump. You won't be kicking a ball in the courtyard for a few days."

"But Mother? I can go up there?"

"Yes. But take things easily, Misha. You can roll your trousers down now." He perched on the edge of his desk and looked at Misha with his kind blue eyes, whose nearsightedness had almost been corrected now by middle-aged farsightedness.

"So . . . this morning you were at one of the gates. Waiting for a chance to cross over?"

Misha nodded. No real point in denying it after Viktor's outburst. Anyway, you couldn't lie to the Doctor.

"Please don't forbid me," he entreated suddenly. And to himself he added, I'd have to go behind your back then, and I don't want to do that.

The Doctor considered and said slowly, "Misha, I can't forbid you to smuggle. I am only too well aware that you are almost fourteen—I almost wish your father had fiddled with your birth certificate as my father fiddled with mine. And I can't hope to succeed where your mother has failed—I know she has tried to dissuade you. All the same," he went on gravely, "I *do* have a responsibility, a duty even, to tell you that Kommissar Auerswald has now decreed that all smugglers, including children, will be summarily shot if they're found on the other side."

A thrill of fear, now quite familiar, rippled down Misha's spine; he felt his thigh burning.

"I'm not *trying* to make things even more difficult for you, Misha, but what I've got to say will do just that. I'm asking you to remember, when you take these risks in order to provide for her, that *your* life is the most precious thing in the world to her—and probably to Rachel, too." This brave David of a man faced a new Goliath every day, almost every hour of his life: If Misha was in himself no giant of a problem, his predicament most certainly was.

"*Great.* Two alternatives. Either way my mother dies, but one way she gets a broken heart as a bonus." Misha spoke bitterly and looked accusingly at his guardian, for who else was there to accuse?

The Doctor slipped off the desk now and stood in front of Misha, his hands firm on the drooping young shoulders. "Misha, we'll do all we can to help Mother—we'll manage somehow without all this extracurricular activity of yours."

But Misha shook his head. "You do all you can as it is, and you're stretched further than your limits already. Anyone can see that. You can't take on parents as well. The children are getting hungrier and hungrier, and you're getting sicker and—well, *sadder*, I suppose—every day." He stopped, afraid that he might have gone too far. The dark thing stirred in his gut, and he wanted to add, And don't get any more sick, Mister Doctor—we all need you to stay alive and strong. But he didn't.

Doctor Korczak was touched that his own afflictions had not escaped this "grandchild" of his.

"Besides," went on Misha, "Mother's too proud to take much more from you."

The Doctor thought sadly of all the humiliating groveling he had done, and still had to do, to beg food for the orphanage. He pointed out quietly, "Pride belongs to the past."

"Dignity, then. Perhaps she has too much dignity."

"No, Misha, you were right the first time. If she refuses help from us, it is out of pride, misplaced and out-of-date. There is no loss of dignity in accepting what is given from love." He paced up and down, his hands behind his back, acutely aware of his young charge's quandary. Misha was quiet, unsure how to reply. He watched the Doctor stop in front of the window—grimy and mended in one or two places with odd-shaped patches of different glass—and look down at the gray and desolate street below.

"How to love a child!" He almost spat out the words he had once used for the title of a book. "How to love a child, indeed! In such an age you love him by trying to stamp out his loyalty to his own mother." He raised his fist at the window in an uncharacteristic gesture of angry defiance. "My God, one day there will be such a reckoning."

At that moment Misha had a desire to go up and embrace his "grandfather," but embarrassment nailed him to the chair. He'd not been bothered by the admiring giggles of the little girls the other night, but now, as he watched the Doctor's distress, his natural loving impulse was paralyzed by embarrassment. Someone told him, much later on, that it is usually the things one doesn't do in life that one regrets, rather than the things one has done and done badly, and it was this scene that was to flash across his mind then and help him to understand the point.

The silence was broken by the younger Monius crying out in his feverish sleep, and the Doctor busied himself with the child.

"Misha, could you fetch me some water, please?" Misha was only too happy to oblige. When he returned, the Doctor was tidying Monius's disheveled blankets.

"I'm all right again now, Misha," he said, smiling in his rather crooked, wistful way. "It was wrong of me to show such vengeance. And whatever you decide—because in the end it has to be your decision—take care."

"I'm sorry, Mister Doctor, I'm really sorry." And he was. Sorry, he thought, for the whole filthy mess, of which his own dilemma was just one tiny part. Nothing that the Doctor had said could or would change the stark fact that his father's remaining belongings had to be sold or exchanged for food, and that the best chance of getting a reasonable deal was on the other side of the wall. But he *was* desperately sorry that, to prevent his mother from starving, he had to torture her with worry and distress the man to whom his family owed their survival. He was aware of how inadequate the expression was: *I'm sorry.* The same thing you said if you stepped on someone's toe.

Doctor Korczak had begun to wipe Monius's face; he stopped and made a swift movement across Misha's own brow with the damp cloth.

"Don't be, my child, don't be. I understand better than you realize. Now run and get those essays finished for me, please."

His editorial work finished, Misha returned a little later to put the pile of paper on the Doctor's desk, and found a slim package, carefully labeled, awaiting him. The folded note said, "Take this to your mother when you visit, with my very kind regards. This is, for once, an instruction and not a request." Then, in brackets and followed by two exclamation marks: "Not even in the ghetto is any day *all* bad!!"

Misha shook his head in amazement. How had the Doctor, with everything else he had to do, found the time to go down to the kitchen, cut off slices of ham, and then to wrap them up as a present so that they couldn't be refused? No, it was true, not even in the ghetto was any day *all* bad.

Even the weather cheered up in the afternoon as Misha walked—or limped—to his mother's room. He was delighted to find her out of bed when he arrived. She was sitting at the table playing a game of solitaire as he let himself in. She had brushed her prematurely gray hair, applied the one stump of lipstick she had left, and, when she smiled at him in welcome, he found it easy to remember how pretty he had once thought she was.

"Look, Mother, a surprise!"

Her smile faded. "Again."

"Yes, and it's a present. You'll really offend Mister Doctor if you refuse. He's been given two enormous hams, much more than he . . ." He stopped in midsentence, aware that that line of pretense was ludicrous. "Anyway," he added, "he insists." Misha handed over the package and eagerly awaited his mother's reaction; she, though, shook her head, unsure how to respond.

"Mother, the Doctor wouldn't have sent it if there weren't enough for all the children to have some first."

"As if you didn't know that smoked ham lasts for weeks. But I will accept. This time only. The occasional potato or cabbage or jar of beets is a wonderful help, but not meat—that's just too precious."

Misha clapped his hands in satisfaction and started picking up the few cooking utensils at random. There were potatoes and carrots left from yesterday, and even two onions that they'd been given by some old family friends who had a tiny vegetable plot in their courtyard by the hospital. Today Mrs. Edelman was going to have a really nourishing meal.

"Misha, let me cook. I'm feeling stronger today."

"No, Mother, I'd like to do it. There'll be days when I can't get here and, anyway, it's fun when there's something decent to put in. I'll stoke up the boiler, but it's so much warmer this week."

"Yes, thank goodness." While the broth simmered, giving off a pleasant and wholesome smell for once, they had a game of cards. Once or twice Misha stole a glance at his mother's face as she studied her cards, and he smiled with a rare contentment.

Presently there was a timid knock on the door. "Come in," called Misha—and nothing happened. He got up and opened it to find four-year-old Sara from the next-door room standing there. She looked up at him, dumbfounded.

"Come in, Sara dear. What can we do for you?"

Picking her way carefully so as to give Misha a wide berth, Sara came into the room and announced, "Mother wants to know if Aunt Lili wants anything."

"Thank her, Sara, very much, but not today. Tell her my son is here and looking after me very well." Sara, oblivious to the pride in Mrs. Edelman's voice, turned and fled from the room as fast as her thin little legs could take her.

"She reminds me of Rachel at that age."

"Yes, she's sweet. But I can't make out what she says with that accent."

"They're very good to me, next door. I wish there were something I could do for them in return."

"Perhaps I'll try and think of something. . . ."

"Oh, no, you won't. I know exactly what that means."

"Mother, don't *worry* so much. I'm incredibly careful, and I don't take silly risks." He turned to the stove then and changed the subject, anxious not to spoil the precarious peace of that happy afternoon together. But he felt he owed her at least another word on the smuggling issue and later, when he had helped her back into bed, tired now and beginning to cough, he patted her on her bony shoulder and said cheerfully, "Mother, there's a saying going the rounds at the moment. They claim there are only three things that are truly invincible: the German army, the British Isles—and Jewish smuggling." He hoped his tone was light and reassuring.

She took his hand in both of hers but didn't smile.

"I won't live to see which one lasts longest, but I pray to God morning, noon, and night that you and Rachel and Eli will." He bent to kiss her cheek, thinking that their mood of contentment had after all been short-lived. But as he left the room, there was one further nice surprise in store for him.

Just as he started to go down the dark narrow stairway, Mrs. Stein came bustling out onto the landing, perfectly timed as usual.

"Misha, we've at last managed to get that great old stove in the basement working, so it'll be much easier to do the laundry. Let me have your mother's sheets from now on, do you hear?"

Misha heard, despite the quaint Southern dialect that was even stronger than her daughter's, and immediately he felt a surge of relief. His mother's laundry had been a problem for months now. Mrs. Stefa had suggested he bring it back to the Orphans' Home, but his mother had stubbornly refused, afraid of imposing any more on the already grossly overburdened orphanage staff. She had herself tried more than once to heat up a pan of water large enough to boil her own sheets, but she was far too weak for the exertion. Once Misha had arrived on an unplanned visit with Rachel, having been accompanied by the Doctor on his way to a begging expedition, and they had found her slumped in a chair, coughing up blood-stained phlegm. From then on he regularly had to summon up all his thirteen-year-old authority to forbid her to try to do it again, but she hated him to do her washing for her, so the increasingly infrequent laundry days had thereafter been marred by their snapping at each other and then feeling guilty about it afterward.

CHAPTER 7

BEFORE GOING TO SLEEP that night, Misha and Viktor planned their bid for the other side in hushed whispers, until eventually they were silenced by Musik, who threw his newspaper-filled pillow at them, swearing crossly. Misha was very worried that Viktor's short sight would be an additional and serious danger: His glasses had splintered a little where they were cracked, and the Doctor had asked him not to wear them anymore.

"I really think I'd better go on my own," Misha had said, without conviction, for the thought was daunting.

"What about your leg? You won't be able to run fast, anyway," Viktor argued.

"Maybe not. But I can dodge in and out of doorways and keep quiet when necessary. You'll be stumbling all over the place without your glasses, Vik."

Viktor was quiet.

"I'm sorry. I know you can't *help* it. But it's silly to take more risks than we have to."

"I don't see why. Anyway, our lives aren't worth much anymore."

"That's wicked, Viktor. Just look at the way Mister Doctor works to keep us all going. And besides, I have to stay alive— for Rachel's and Eli's sakes."

It was the last argument that finally persuaded Viktor that discretion would be the better part of valor. Or maybe it gave him an honorable way of opting out without losing face. Misha did not know and didn't mind which; he couldn't see his friend's expression in the dim light of the dormitory, closely huddled though they were.

And so next morning they ate a silent breakfast together, before Misha, his bruised leg now really stiff and painful, limped off in search of Rachel.

"Where's Rachel?" he asked Roza, who was preparing her corner of the girls' dormitory for the day's activities.

"Down with Elena. I think she has a bit of fever, Misha."

"Who, Rachel?"

"Elena."

Misha blushed. "Thanks, Roza." His progress back down the stairs was slow, and not helped by bumping into the six-year-old Goldstein twins who were busy quarreling with each other. Hanne laughed in her wheezy, asthmatic way as she clasped the two howling little boys to her and told them not to be so rough with Misha.

Misha wasn't really looking where he was going. His leg was painful, but he was also aware of a different ache, rather less easy to identify. He had always been troubled by his lack of warm, spontaneous affection toward Elena, even though he understood that this lack belonged in some obscure way to the grief that had haunted him since his father's premature death. Just now he had experienced an unmistakable glow of relief when Roza had said it was Elena and not Rachel who had the fever, but it was a glow that turned almost instantly to shame.

"Oh, Misha, *there* you are." He had entered the "nursery" next to Mrs. Stefa's room, where Rachel was trying to extricate herself from Elena's arms. "Thank goodness you've come. I have to help upstairs, and she needs company all the time when she's not well. Are you all right?"

"Yes, of course." Misha avoided her gaze and stooped over Elena's cot. As so often when he looked at his small sister, he was conscious of a nostalgia that fluttered in his heart like an imprisoned bird. She was so uncannily like their father, so disturbingly like pictures he had seen of himself at the same age. He lifted her up against his shoulder and self-consciously pecked one flushed and blotchy cheek.

"Meca, eca!" she crowed, spreading her fingers against his mouth in welcome.

Rachel shook her head and laughed. "You always get a better welcome than I do—it's not fair." And with that she was gone.

She didn't even notice my limp, reflected Misha, just a little wistfully. He walked around carrying Elena, her head resting unusually inert on his shoulder, and looked at the other babies and toddlers. He had stopped by the cot of undersized, unresponsive Josef, whose brain had been damaged by falling masonry in the September 1939 air raids, when Mrs. Stefa bustled in.

"Oh, Misha, there you are. Her temperature is a bit lower this morning, but she's not too well, as you can see."

Misha nodded, not liking to ask how high it had been the previous evening when he, busy planning with Viktor, had been too preoccupied to come and nurse her. No wonder Rachel had sounded reproachful just now.

"Could you take her up to be weighed and measured quickly now, Misha? The Doctor's running late this morning, and we'll never be ready for the Children's Court at this rate."

Misha's heart missed a beat. The Children's Court! How could he have forgotten? He would have to tell Rachel what his plan was, for otherwise she would be sure to miss him in court and start asking questions. The court met every Saturday, and the five judges—children who had drawn lots—meted out punishment to other children who had committed misdemeanors, in strict accordance with Doctor Korczak's Code of Laws, compiled for his orphanages years ago during the other Great War.

Misha glanced at the clock on the wall. Ten minutes past eight. He ought to be taking up his position opposite Twarda Street gate at eight-thirty. There was no time to lose. But he couldn't possibly refuse Mrs. Stefa's request. Obediently he carried Elena out of the room and up the stairs, at a loss to know what to do. When he saw the line outside the Doctor's room, his heart sank. Perhaps Eli could be weighed and measured tomorrow? No, the Doctor was so meticulous he'd be bound to notice. Perhaps he could cut in line? Not a chance. Both Adziu and Musik were in front and neither of them would willingly give way, that was certain. Then, to his surprise, Roza brushed past and, seeing Misha standing there, said, "I don't think Eli ought to wait, since she's got a fever. I'll take her from you, Misha. I'm sure there are things you could do for Mrs. Stefa downstairs." And Roza, angel that she was, removed Elena—always one of her favorites—from his arms. He stopped only to stutter his thanks and to pat the baby rather awkwardly on the head, before turning away as fast as he could.

Hovering near the back door into the yard was Viktor, looking somehow more anxious and unsure of himself than ever, holding his damaged glasses.

"Oh, I wish I was coming with you."

"I *bet* you do." Misha managed a grin. He patted the waistband of his trousers. Yes, the belts were there, and the wallets and cuff links were tucked carefully inside what passed for a jacket.

"Well, wish me luck."

"G'luck, Misha."

Misha walked through the yard, dodging someone's ball; then, when he'd reached the gate, he turned and half ran back, grimacing at the stiffness in his bad leg. Viktor was still at the door; the children on kitchen duty were already behind him, milling around the sinks.

"Viktor, if anything happens to me, look after Mother and Rachel and Eli." The boys shook hands soberly. Misha knew Viktor could do nothing to help his mother or his sisters, but he felt as if he were in some way discharging an important duty. Viktor, for his part, knew perfectly well how powerless he was, and he knew that Misha knew, too; yet he felt somehow honored, entrusted with such an important responsibility.

□   □   □

It took Misha ten minutes to reach the houses opposite the Twarda Street gate. This was probably going to be the hardest and most dangerous part of the whole enterprise. He certainly didn't share Viktor's confidence in the good intentions of Henryk, the "friendly" guard to whom he owed his aching leg. And even if Henryk had been at all well disposed toward Viktor because of their family friendship in the past, it was unlikely that these feelings would be transferred to Misha, especially after his insolence the day before. But it was the only way. He had to give it a try.

In any event, Misha was lucky. The return of the night shift from the other side brought a disturbance in the form of a woman who was having some sort of fit on the open truck. With much shouting and stamping and pushing and prodding of rifle butts, the sentry police, both German and Jewish, seemed preoccupied with the night workers, and it was relatively easy for Misha to slip through while the gates were open. He was not the only one to do so, either, nor the youngest. One little urchin with huge holes in his short pants couldn't have been more than six years old. Misha didn't waste any time watching the proceedings in the truck, but he couldn't help noticing that Viktor's "friend" was as active as any of them with his rifle butt.

Remembering just in time to rip off his arm band, Misha made his way quickly through the now only half-familiar streets to his former home. Now that he had crossed into "the promised land," he felt cheerful and oddly confident that the old family friends he planned to visit, the Kolakowskis, would be able and willing to help him. It didn't occur to him that he might frighten or bring trouble on them by appearing on their doorstep, for like most ghetto children he tended to think that everyone on the other side of the wall lived a secure and unthreatened life. He was chiefly aware of a rather unfamiliar sense of anticipation and hope. But that was to be short-lived.

Turning the corner into Okopowa Street, he looked eagerly for the Kolakowskis' house. He saw it; he stopped; he stared.

The house, which, for the last twenty-four hours had in his mind's eye come to represent comfort or even rescue, could now offer nothing. The first two floors of the narrow terraced property that the family had occupied were windowless; the front door had been boarded up, and a notice printed in German, which Misha couldn't read, had been pasted on at a haphazard angle. Beside it was a tattered poster advertising a performance of the Warsaw ballet back in November. There were, he noticed as he walked gingerly right up to the front doorsteps, bullet holes in the brickwork around the door. On the third floor one of the still-intact windows was half-open, and a curtain fluttered in the spring breeze.

Perhaps, he thought, with a quickening of hope . . . but, no, the house had no usable entrance. When he looked up again, he could see that the curtain was badly torn. He stood forlornly staring at the house for several minutes before becoming fully aware of how vulnerable he was. Twice he was bumped into and once sworn at, for Okopowa Street was busy at that time of day, though deserted compared with the streets in the ghetto.

Just as well I'm not Jewish to look at, he thought after the second bump, but all the same he felt decidedly too conspicuous for comfort. He had to make up his mind what to do without delay. So, accepting the fact that he wasn't going to find the Kolakowskis, he found himself making straight for the small park at the end of the street, a familiar place and now, to the ghetto boy starved for the sight of greenery, a sort of haven. The little public garden was already occupied. One or two ragged old men sat on the spring grass, their backs against tree trunks; three equally old but not quite so unkempt women sat gossiping on a bench with a broken back; and a couple of young mothers walked up and down the overgrown central path pushing their baby carriages. Misha thought of the few tiny green areas, sandwiched between some of the courtyards over in the ghetto, where mothers had to pay the equivalent of a loaf of bread to buy a couple of hours' fresh air for their babies. He found himself a place under a cherry tree, and thought, too, how excited some of the very young children in the orphanage would have been to see a fruit tree in blossom in real life.

How can it be so beautiful despite everything, he wondered. I suppose Nature doesn't really care. He thought of Rachel's geranium cuttings and wondered whether they would flower in time for their mother's birthday as Rachel so fervently hoped.

He noticed several children hanging around the other entrance to the park; they kept stopping passersby with what looked, to a boy used to ghetto begging conditions, like a reasonable degree of success. In a flash of inspiration, Misha knew what he should do next. He had lost his outlet for smuggling, so he would beg instead.

All the same, he went on watching the other children, loath to leave the comparative safety of his vantage point. It was comforting to feel the tree trunk against his back. He wondered anxiously whether they would allow him to join them, and scrutinized each one as well as he could to make sure he didn't recognize any of them.

Eventually he could stand the suspense no longer. More than ever aware of the ache in his bruised thigh, he walked slowly up to one of the boys—a redhead not unlike Viktor to look at— and said as casually as his thumping heart would allow, "I've had to change my spot—SS patrols. Okay if I share yours just for this morning?"

The redheaded boy looked at Misha curiously, and after a few moments shrugged his shoulders in a gesture of compliance. None of the others—four children between about age nine and twelve—took much notice of him. Misha was surprised at their lack of concern at being asked to share their spot with a total stranger, but he didn't have long to wait before he discovered the reason. The Viktor-like boy had just offered to share some apples with him, telling him to hide them quickly in his sleeve, and Misha was just wondering what he had done to deserve such generosity when two large thugs of about seventeen or eighteen arrived, carrying a couple of brown paper sacks.

"Come on, then, hand over, you scum," they demanded roughly. The others, all much younger and smaller, meekly put their bits and pieces into the bags without a word of protest: it obviously came as no surprise to them. Misha didn't want to draw attention to himself, so decided to follow suit and part with the apples he'd just been given, though it hurt him to do so. He wondered when Rachel and Eli had last had a fresh apple.

He was just about to shake his sleeve over the bag's gaping mouth when the larger of the two youths gave a yell.

"My God, that's Michal Edelman. Stinking little Yid. I'd recognize him anywhere." Misha looked into the youth's face for just an instant, but long enough to recognize the elder brother of a boy who used to be in his class at school. He had always been a bully; Misha remembered how he had been one of the ringleaders of Jewhunts and Jewbaiting games even then.

"What the hell are you doing here, you filthy Jewscum?" he roared.

Misha didn't wait to hear more. Dropping the apples, he turned and fled, as unaware of direction and destination as of the ache in his leg. He was mindful only of the shouts and steps behind him, which seemed to be almost on his heels. He knew that he had to dodge his pursuers immediately if he were to survive; it would only be a matter of moments before other passersby were alerted and he would—probably literally—be hounded to death. Fear gave him speed, but his heart was hammering wildly, and he ran blindly and without a plan. Suddenly, around a corner the surroundings became familiar. He was in Krochmalna Street, where the orphanage had been before it had to move inside the ghetto wall—Misha had sometimes visited a friend there whose mother had died. He saw some huge cans just inside a courtyard and, without pausing to consider, dodged behind one of them and cowered there, his breath heaving painfully in his chest, until he heard the two youths racing past. He stayed there for a long time, becoming almost frozen after the heat and panic had subsided, unable to think what to do next. He must have stayed there for almost three hours, unperturbed by the smelliness of the huge trash cans that had saved him. When his wits did begin to return, he felt furious with himself for abandoning three perfectly good apples that he would have been only too glad of now. Must be quite an organized gang of beggars, he thought to himself. I never realized it happened over on this side, too.

Eventually Misha plucked up enough courage to peep out and then, when he was confident that the street was quiet, walked gingerly along the pavement, keeping close to the houses. He had nearly given up all hope of begging, but when he got to the corner of Krochmalna and Wronia streets, an old man in the produce store was outside rearranging his display; before Misha knew what was happening, he heard himself say, "Have you any fruit to spare?"

The man stopped and looked at him curiously. "Why on earth should I do that for you, sonny? Every other kid who comes by here is hungry, so what makes *you* so special?"

"Because I've got these to offer you," replied Misha in a rush, totally without forethought. He pulled his father's silver cuff links from his pocket and held them out to the old man. He should have known better after two years in the ghetto jungle. The grocer made a grab at them, dropped one on the floor, and though they both made to pick it up, was quicker than Misha. He pocketed them without another glance, then tore off some newspaper and hurriedly filled it with some carrots and beets, three potatoes, and—perhaps as a concession to guilt—two shining red apples. "Go on, take these, and clear off." Misha eyed some large ripe-looking pears and was very tempted to grab, but his experience earlier that day had taught him some caution, so he turned and walked away, sick at his own foolishness.

Now he was really at a loss to know what to do next. He had no idea what the time was, but remembered there was a clock in Kazimierza Place, which at least gave him somewhere to aim for. Terrified that he'd be recognized again, he tried to keep his head down, but as a result he bumped into two passersby. When he got to the clock, it registered only just after two o'clock, which was depressing because it seemed so much later to him. He'd have to while away four hours before he could even hope to get back into the ghetto. He wondered if the clock was wrong but then spotted another one on a church tower, which told him the same thing.

CHAPTER 8

ALTHOUGH MISHA WAS ANXIOUS to get as close to the Twarda Street gate as possible and avoid any more confrontations, he was bitterly disappointed that his expedition hadn't been successful. The lumpy little packet of carrots, beets, potatoes, and two apples under his arm felt hard, like a reproach; surely there was one more thing he could try? He stood in the doorway of an abandoned shop, reading some old and peeling handbills about concerts, interspersed with scrawled Nazi slogans, when he suddenly remembered that Jan, who had worked as an apprentice for his father, lived just off Kazimierza Place, with a rather nice elderly father, his mother having died when he was a boy. Now that *could* be a possibility. What was his address? Misha looked around him, trying to recover his bearings. Surely Jan'll help if he can, thought Misha. He couldn't think why it hadn't occurred to him before. Unless they were no longer there, of course. He remembered how his mother would send him down to the workshop on errands for "the two Jans" in the days before the ghetto.

He found the little alleyway tucked away behind the square after only one false start. He hovered around on the cobblestones, trying to remember which tenement building it was. A middle-aged woman with a very lined face came out of one and asked him who he wanted. The place seemed strangely quiet and deserted.

"Oh, old Mr. . . ." Misha felt so stupid, unable to remember the surname he had once known so well. He cursed his nerves and hoped he didn't appear as scared as he felt. But the woman seemed preoccupied with problems of her own and only waved vaguely at one of the houses.

"The young men have all gone, anyway. There's an old fellow

on the top floor there. Perhaps that's him." And she walked on, her shoulders hunched. Misha walked into the cool, dark, dilapidated hallway that somehow smelled of brown. It was very quiet. He stood still and listened. He heard a distant door bang and felt himself start; then, quiet again. It was the right house, though: he recognized the ugly mirror in the hall and the colored glass in the front door. He walked up the dark, peeling stairway, his heart thumping in its familiar rhythm of fear. There was no obvious sign of life on the first two floors—such a contrast to all the houses in the ghetto, which teemed with humanity of every shape and size and age. On the top landing Misha's nose registered the unmistakable smell of cooking sauerkraut. He knocked softly on the shabby wooden door. No answer. He knocked again. Still no response. Perhaps he's frightened to answer, he thought. He knocked again, loudly this time, listening apprehensively to the echo. This time he heard footsteps shuffling toward the door. Slowly it creaked open to reveal Jan's father, older and smaller than ever. He was entirely bald, a fact that somehow accentuated his large, prominent nose. He was wearing rather dirty trousers above stockinged feet. One thing that was not old and decrepit about him, though, was his eyes—large, clear and gray—which, after a few moments of narrowed scrutiny, lit up in recognition.

"Good gracious, it's Misha. Come in, my boy." He put a hand on Misha's shoulder and practically pulled him inside, shutting the door quickly behind him and making a point of careful bolting. "Just a precaution—you never know these days." He looked at Misha and then clasped the boy's shoulders between wrinkled hands in a gesture of welcome. He kept shaking his head.

"Well, I never, I never—I never thought to see you again, my boy. Come in and tell me how you all are. How's your dad?"

Misha realized with a start just how out of touch the old man was. He led Misha into a dingy sort of parlor, where a little table was carefully laid with a place for one, and sat Misha down in the one armchair.

"Stay there, child. I'll get you something to drink." And he came back with a glass of something alcoholic, although it could have been anything as far as Misha's inexperienced palate was concerned. Misha then had to give a summary of everything that had happened to the family since the day they had left for the ghetto.

When he'd finished, he stopped rather abruptly and asked, "But what about Jan? Where is he?"

The old man's face suddenly became smaller.

"They took him off to Germany. He's in an armaments factory near Berlin." He paused. "He's all right . . . I think. I've actually had two letters." He patted his trouser pocket, and Misha realized that he must carry them around with him for reassurance. He was silent, not really knowing what to say, and the old man stared into the middle distance, lost in thought.

Then he rubbed his hands and jumped up. "But I'll get you something to eat. You must be starving. I'm so sorry."

"No, no, not really," but Misha's protest was entirely unconvincing. He got up and followed Jan's father into the tiny kitchen. It was spotlessly clean and tidy. A dish of sauerkraut stood on the hob, still steaming.

"Do you like eggs?"

Misha opened his eyes wide. It seemed such a silly question. How could anyone not like eggs?

Uncle Lek, for Misha suddenly remembered that was what he and Rachel used to call him, took down three large eggs from a wooden rack and broke them into a bowl. Misha wanted to tell him not to share his meager rations but somehow couldn't bring himself to. He felt the saliva rise from the bottom of his mouth; his stomach churned in anticipation. He watched, fascinated, as Uncle Lek beat the eggs to a froth.

"My sister. She lives outside Warsaw and keeps hens. Sometimes she manages to get in to see me, but the buses don't run properly anymore." Misha felt glad that Uncle Lek's sister was still around.

In ten minutes they were sitting opposite each other, a second neat little place setting having been laid. Uncle Lek had found onions and herbs for the omelette that, together with the sauerkraut and potatoes he'd already prepared for his own solitary meal, made the most delicious dinner that Misha could remember. It was washed down with a sweet, cloudy, homemade apple juice, another gift from Lek's sister in the country. And when Misha had finished, still hungry but more nearly full than he had been for many a month, Lek went over to the heavy, dark sideboard, from where a crucifix and photos of Jan and his dead mother dominated the little room, opened a cupboard, and brought out a small red-patterned tin.

"Jan always liked a sweet after a special dinner. I keep a few in case he comes back unexpectedly." He held out the tin to his young guest and said anxiously, "Take several. Take a few back to Rachel—I bet she's changed a bit. Just leave a couple, that's all."

Misha didn't know what to do. He peered at the familiar-shaped fruit drops and then up at the kind, wrinkled old face, which was nodding vigorously at him. Then he took a handful in a quick, decisive gesture, but as quickly dropped some to make sure of leaving several behind. He put them in his pocket, then looked anxiously at the clock on the mantelpiece.

"Uncle Lek, I have to try and get back over the wall with the six o'clock shift. I'm sorry."

"You could stay here, Misha. No one would think of searching this place for you."

Misha paused, tempted for a minute.

Then he blushed. "No, no, there's Mother. And Rachel and Eli."

"Yes, of course."

Misha suddenly felt the need for haste. The old man, his hands at his sides, his face smiling sadly, stood awkwardly by the parlor door. In a clumsy gesture that surprised them both, Misha went up to him and leaned his head against a wizened shoulder. He felt a gentle hand pat his hair, and he thought of the Doctor.

"It was the best meal I've ever had. And I hope Jan comes back soon."

Then, with eyes stinging and throat aching, he pulled himself away and stood by the front door as Uncle Lek unbolted it at the top and bottom to let him go.

"May God go with you, child." They shook hands briefly; then Misha turned and disappeared down the dark narrow stairs, aware of his bad leg again for the first time since entering the building.

He found his way to the junction with Chmielna and Zelazna streets again, but as he was about to turn north, he heard the sound of marching. He pressed himself into a doorway, praying that the occupants of the house wouldn't appear, and waited, his heart once again doing overtime. He shivered, remembering the marching he'd heard on the Night of Blood and the crumpled heap that had been the baker and his son. The rhythmic sounds seemed to get nearer, and he was convinced that the patrol would turn into Chmielna Street and pass within full view. That would surely be the end. The beating of his heart mingled with the marching of the invisible boots and reached a unified crescendo. Misha came as near to fainting as he had ever done; his head was one great drumbeat.

But the eternal moment eventually passed, the marching receded into the distance, and once again the street was quiet. An old woman in black shuffled by within a couple of meters but didn't appear to notice him. However, it was time to move again; cowering in doorways was a suspicious activity. Misha walked along the pavement, his hands deep in his pockets, trying to look nonchalant and unconcerned. He got as near to the Twarda Street gate as he could and then wondered how he was going to kill time within sight of the gate without looking conspicuous. He was very aware of his ragged clothes, though he'd seen plenty of children on this side, too, with holes in their trousers. He felt the weight of his father's belts, and tears of frustration mixed with disappointment pricked at his eyes. He couldn't have asked old Uncle Lek, who had so freely shared his meager rations with him. The whole foolish adventure had been in vain—it might even yet cost him his life, for all he knew. In any case, he was beginning not to care very much anymore; he almost longed for the sordid familiarity of the ghetto, the—extraordinary idea—comparative safety of anonymity in a crowd. Well, at least he had a few vegetables that would keep his mother going for a couple of days.

Perhaps he'd spent longer with Uncle Lek than he realized, for he didn't have as long to wait as he expected. Soon he heard the telltale rolling, the shouts, the barked orders. The day shift was going home.

He crept nearer until he was just a few meters behind the truck. He couldn't hope for the sort of diversion that had enabled him to slip over so easily in the morning. He looked up and found himself staring into several dull, exhausted faces. Then before he knew what he was doing, he had stretched out his arms and was being hauled up by several pairs of willing hands. It wasn't until he was safely huddled among his rescuers that he recognized one of the men from his mother's building.

"Got some loot then, son?" he whispered, eyeing the bulge in Misha's shirt.

Misha shook his head sadly. "Nothing worth having really— just a few carrots and beets. Please don't tell Mother—she worries so."

The young man nodded his assent, but Misha noticed uneasily that he continued to eye his bulging shirt. Soon another truck umbered up behind, and then another. The yelling started and stopped again with the arrival of each one; then, when the convoy was complete, the great gate swung open, and they lurched forward. There wasn't such strict counting on the way in, and Misha was in luck again; tonight it was the second truck that was chosen for the search. He was merely unloaded with the others in the front truck and in a few minutes was making his way back down Twarda Street in the direction of the Orphans' Home.

When he got to the doorway that had sheltered Viktor and him two days before—it seemed to him a year before—he couldn't resist looking back. There, a little smuggler, maybe six or seven years old, was being searched by an SS thug and a blue policeman. He had to open up his shirt and turn out his pockets. He'd managed to get hold of some oranges that were, of course, snatched away, before he was chased down the street while being beaten by a rifle butt. The child screamed, and Misha could see blood running down his face. He stood in silence for a few moments before turning into Sienna Street, aware that he had not, after all, been so unlucky.

CHAPTER 9

THERE WAS NO ONE to welcome Misha when he got back to the orphanage. The kitchen was deserted for once, as nearly everyone was involved in a rehearsal of Tagore's *Post*, a play that was to be produced for the ghetto public later in the summer, in the hope of raising funds for the home.

Misha was hungry again. He made straight for one of the huge cauldrons cooling on the hob, full of Mrs. Stefa's newly made beet marmalade. Picking up a spoon and dipping it into the mixture, he watched a skin wrinkle and crease across the surface of the liquid. He lifted the spoon sideways and studied the way the marmalade converged toward a central point before trickling off the edge, until it coagulated into one last globule that stubbornly refused to drop. The sticky, translucent substance together with the smell of bread—even plastery ghetto bread—made him grin in deep and unexpected contentment at being home, and alive.

A noise made him turn suddenly, guiltily dropping the ladle into the marmalade.

"Misha! Thank God! How did it go?" It was Viktor, all anxious concern and freckled frown.

"It's great to be back. I'll tell you all about it later."

"Oh, Misha—that's not fair. Did you see the Kolakowskis? Did Henryk let you over? What did you get? Come on, tell me."

Misha realized that he was not going to be let off that easily. He patted his bulging pouch rather sadly and, to get it over with quickly, admitted, "Nothing much, I'm afraid. In fact, in one way the whole expedition was pretty useless. Come on—let's go up the back stairs. I need to put these away. I'll tell you the whole story up there."

After Misha's adventure, life at the Orphans' Home continued more or less as before. He visited his mother daily, and he and Rachel, but especially Rachel, spent a good deal of time carrying Elena up and down the courtyard in the May sunshine. The virus had left her weak and listless, but she was fretful when left alone. Mister Doctor thought it better that she should miss one or two visits to her mother, which made Mrs. Edelman very anxious, and she bombarded Rachel and Misha with questions about her temperature and other details.

"You wouldn't hide anything from me, would you?" she asked accusingly, fearing the worst.

While helping in the room that Eli shared with the other toddlers, Rachel told Mrs. Stefa about her mother's suspicions. Mrs. Stefa passed them on to the Doctor, who decided to accompany all three children to the gloomy room on Orla Street the next day.

"Here she is at last. Perhaps I was being overcautious." He smiled as he handed over the child, who was already straining to be out of his arms and onto the floor. She was quite chirpy again, in any case, having regained some strength from a special orphanage porridge—groats mixed with horse blood and sweetened with synthetic honey. The Doctor trudged off on one of his begging errands while the children stayed with their mother.

On Sunday nights the *Home Gazette* continued to be read aloud at the little ritual that had been observed in the orphanage for over twenty years. Misha listened with pride when Rachel, a regular and prolific contributor both of imaginary stories and comments on orphanage matters, read out her offerings in her gruff little voice. He particularly liked one of her stories, and, while editing it the previous week, had shown it to Viktor.

"Quite good, for a girl," Viktor had said hesitantly, anxious to please but not really sure what Misha wanted to hear. The story was about an apple tree that, one spring, was so worried about the children slowly dying of starvation, who belonged to the house and garden where it grew, that it forgot to flower and could therefore produce no fruit for them in the autumn.

The Children's Court continued to sit every Saturday, and the week after Misha's adventure a case of bullying among the nine- and ten-year-old boys was brought by Miss Hannia, who worked as a nurse in the orphanage. Tiny Stefan, not only undersized but also prematurely gray, was being made to hand over half his daily ration of bread to buy immunity from beatings by Musik and his "gang." It was only when Stefan became ill and began talking in his feverish sleep that the matter came to light. The Doctor himself had taken the unusual step of summoning them to the isolation room to tell them that they had behaved like barbarians—one of his severest reprimands—and the five judges on the panel, sitting around the table covered in its special green baize cloth, took an equally dim view. Two of them, Regina and Julek, favored expulsion from the orphanage, but they were outnumbered: That extreme measure had only been invoked twice, under Paragraph 1,000 of the Code, in twenty-five years.

Misha, who had not been charged for leaving the orphanage on his smuggling escapade—although Mrs. Stefa had argued with the Doctor that he should be, to deter any of the others "with the same foolish idea"—was elected to the panel that day. He knew a bit about Musik and guessed at what might lie behind his tough, bully-boy exterior. Unlike most of the children at the Orphans' Home who had lost one or both parents through death, Musik had been abandoned by his very young, terrified, and unmarried mother a few months after the invasion. He had made his own way to the orphanage, starving and very frightened, early in 1940 when the orphanage was still in Krochmalna Street. It was almost impossible to like Musik, who seemed to have no redeeming qualities, but the Doctor had once asked his older children, in their evening discussion class, to imagine how they would feel if their mothers, instead of being taken from them by death, had gone away and left them to their fate alone and unprotected. At the time Misha had been consumed with longing for his own lost father, and the Doctor's remarks had made a big impression on him: For the first time he had begun to see that some people had worse problems than he did.

Remembering this now, he reminded the other judges that Musik never tried to deny or lie about the things he did wrong, and that expelling him from the orphanage was hardly likely to reform his character. He persuaded Genia, Rachel's serious-minded friend, who said she agreed that Musik needed help rather than punishment.

"What about poor little Stefan?" demanded blue-eyed Regina. Misha had to restrain a smile when he saw how her face had become even prettier with a flush of righteous indignation. He had always had a soft spot for Regina and sometimes dreamed that one day they would be married and live in a nice house with a garden in Praga, one of Warsaw's smart suburbs. His mother and sisters, he liked to imagine, would live next door—but he had never consulted Regina on any of his plans!

"Stefan will get help, and I don't think this is likely to happen again." Genia's tone was prim and cold—she had seen the look of admiration on Misha's face as he watched Regina. "I think the Court should rule Paragraph 900. That way Musik will have to learn to be responsible toward someone else." In the end the Court's verdict was unanimous, and under Paragraph 900 Musik was ordered to find an older child to be his supervisor during a sort of probation period. If the Court ordered any punishments during the time of probation, they would be given to the supervisor and not to Musik. Misha looked at Musik's face as he stood there in front of all the assembled children, searching for signs of remorse or relief, but he could find neither.

Through all the day-to-day activities that made up the life of the Orphans' Home, there was one question that hovered con-

stantly at the back of Misha's mind. The picture of his so obviously dying mother was with him almost continuously; on the
one hand he wanted with all his heart to sell his few remaining
possessions to make her last weeks more comfortable, but on
the other he dared not risk alarming her by an unusual or pro-
longed absence. He was terrified that even if he did succeed in
getting over to the other side again, he might not next time be
able to get back. And not to be close at hand, when the time
came, was unthinkable.

He was just formulating an unpromising scheme for selling his
things within the ghetto through one of the Nazi-controlled
shops when, one evening, the Doctor summoned him to the isolation room. He had some news for him that was to push the
issue of food smuggling, for the time being, anyway, to the very
back of his mind.

Faithful to his promise to Mrs. Edelman, Doctor Korczak
had, with the help of one or other of his secret Aryan contacts,
arranged for baby Elena to be taken over to the other side and
looked after by a non-Jewish Polish family. He never divulged
how he had managed it, either to Misha or his mother, or said
whether money had changed hands. There were certain things,
for all his approachability and frequent playfulness, that one did
not ask the Doctor.

Misha now learned that he himself was to play a crucial role in
Elena's escape. It would arouse suspicion, Korczak explained, if
he, a figure well-known to many of the Jewish and Polish police,
were seen lingering anywhere near the wall with one individual
child. It could hardly be passed off as an orphanage outing—
something that never took place now, in any case.

The Doctor had, characteristically, put a lot of thought into
the plan before even mentioning it to Misha. He had enlisted
the help of Sabina, the Home's seamstress, whose practical common sense, he thought, would help her to cope with the unpre-
dictable. Elena was to be taken to Kozla Alley, home of the

ghetto's most professional large-scale smuggling activities. There, at a given time, she would be hoisted up in an improvised cradle—like so much flour—to a window on the second floor at the back of one of the Aryan-occupied houses, whose front doors looked out onto Freta Street on the other side. Most of these windows had been grated to prevent just such things from taking place, but the grating would be removed at the prearranged moment. It was thus vital to get the timing exactly right, even though conditions in the crowded, lawless streets of the ghetto were such that precision timing could not be guaranteed. It had been a condition of the agreement that Korczak say nothing to Misha about the prospective foster family, in case he should be caught and interrogated under torture. All the Doctor could say was that the family had at one time been grateful patients and had always remained in touch with him, despite all the obvious barriers and dangers. It was a Monday when Korczak broke the news to Misha, and the transfer was to take place on the following Wednesday.

"So it would be a good idea for you to take Elena to see your mother today or tomorrow. We can't risk leaving it until the last minute on Wednesday, though I know that's her usual day."

"Does Mother know?" Misha was already anticipating her anguish.

"She knows that I've been trying to arrange something. But she doesn't know that the date and time have been fixed, and it's probably better if it stays that way, Misha." Misha nodded dumbly, unsure whether it would be best for his mother to know or not. But he was aware of a sense of pride at being trusted and confided in over something so important, and he remembered the intention he'd avowed on the Night of Blood in April, after the Bergsons had been murdered, to be as worthy as he possibly could of the Doctor's example. It wasn't going to be easy.

"I'll try and take you all up there this afternoon, after your rest time," Korczak went on. He placed both hands on Misha's shoulders and smiled his lopsided smile. "It's a gamble, Michal. You know too much for me to hide that from you. But I earnestly believe that it's the best thing for Eli." He needn't have said it; Misha knew full well that the Doctor would never lightly take such a gamble on a child's life. But to consider why it should be necessary to take such risks made dangerously restless the thing deep within him, for it forced him to imagine what might be in store for the rest of them.

CHAPTER 10

On Wednesday, June 10, Doctor Korczak was, as usual, up early. As usual, he had worked late into the night adding to his memoirs, poring over his medical charts, writing begging letters; as usual, he had slept a fretful sleep, always dimly aware of the murmurings of feverish children, Felunia at the moment and Julek, who had taken little Monius's place. He could no longer hide from himself the fact that he was ill, seriously so; yet he had to keep going. Years before, when he had gone as a soldier in the Polish army to the front lines of the other Great War, Mrs. Stefa had kept the orphanage running like clockwork—according to his guidelines certainly, but in his total physical absence. That would no longer be possible. She could not be mother, nurse, doctor, administrator, and provider to nearly two hundred children who were dying, quite literally, from oppression. These days the Orphans' Home was more like an old people's home than an orphanage. Sometimes he even made a joke of this to the children themselves, asking at breakfast, "Who's feeling worst today?" And then the children would start comparing their temperatures.

But this morning he tended his geraniums with an even heavier heart. The plan he had worked out for baby Elena was elaborate, but far from foolproof. As he bent his bald head over the window box, parting leaves, snipping and watering, he worried about things going wrong. Even suppose it all went smoothly, how strange and frightening it would be for Eli to be surrounded by total strangers.

This was a comparatively good time of day in the ghetto. Below him Sienna Street was quiet, and the cool of night had to some degree lessened the fetid smell of disease and decay that would later in the day invade the air they breathed. He noticed an SS guard watching him from across the street; he was young and apparently just curious. The Doctor found himself wondering if he were freshly arrived from home in Germany, even whether he missed his family. Then he went on to wonder how long it would be before the youth—surely no more than nineteen or twenty—would join in with the general brutality, with the hunting, the beating, the killing.

Quietly he checked the sick children, none of whom were yet awake. He opened a drawer of his desk and carefully removed a brown envelope. He crept down the stairs to the nursery, where he was not surprised to find Mrs. Stefa already up and about. She was neatly folding a pile of little clothes onto one of the tables, whose legs had been sawn off long ago to make it the right height for toddlers' activities. The Doctor had always been a great believer in adapting furniture to suit the needs of his charges. Mrs. Stefa had laid out the two beautifully smocked cotton nightgowns that had once been Rachel's and that had come into the orphanage with the Edelman children. There was a lovely handmade shawl, too, an old family prayer book, and a chewed and once-treasured rattle. Beside these Mrs. Stefa had laid one or two items from her dwindling linen store—two or three small towels, leggings, a woolly jacket, and a couple of faded little dresses. The nicest dress she had set aside for Elena to wear; ironically, it was white with a pattern of tiny blue stars. Mrs. Stefa saw the Doctor looking at it dubiously.

"They're all right, aren't they? Not too like the Stars of David?"

"No, Stefa, they'll do. The connection would be far too subtle for any Nazi."

There were clean blue socks to match laid out, and some lovingly polished red shoes. Young Jakob, whose father had been a cobbler, had become really quite skilled at producing decent footwear from the remnants of worn-out leather shoes. The Doctor watched his companion work, puttering backward and forward between the cupboard and the table. They had been partners for far too long to feel the need for small talk. He noticed, pinned to the woolly jacket, the brooch he himself had brought back for Stefa from his second trip to Palestine. It was a sort of aquamarine set in pretty silver filigree. He remembered how shyly he had handed it over, afraid that the delicate little object might not after all appeal to the big, plain woman, with the matter-of-fact manner. He always forgot, when he was away from her, just how masculine her looks were. He remembered how pleased he had been at her obvious delight. He knew that it was one of the few things of any value she had left, and the fact that she was now giving it in farewell to baby Elena was, he understood, a measure of the hope she was investing in the child's future.

Presently Elena herself woke up and, hauling herself up against the bars of the crib, pointed at the things and said again and again, "Eli dwess, Eli dwess." That, of course, was the cue for the other babies to start stirring, and the Doctor and Mrs. Stefa busied themselves getting them up and dressed. Before Mrs. Stefa shepherded the toddlers into the kitchen, she said tersely to Korczak, "I've got a bag for her, but I thought Michal and Rachel should see what she was taking before I packed it."

Before long Rachel appeared in the kitchen. "Please, can I have my breakfast with Eli today, Mrs. Stefa?"

"Of course you can, pet. Sit yourself down—oh, and see that Adam's bread actually gets to his mouth, will you?"

Misha had had the same idea as Rachel. He came into the kitchen just in time to see her putting her own share of synthetic honey onto their little sister's bread. He smiled, for he had done exactly the same thing the day before. Why just yesterday, though, he thought, with that particular chagrin that wells up into the hole left by things undone. He sat down heavily on Rachel's other side with a brief "Morning." He rubbed his eyes; it had been a very bad night.

Elena clambered across Rachel toward her brother, talking gibberish fast and furiously. She was now as well as any of the children at the Orphans' Home: hollow cheeked, pale, and heavy-lidded still, but with a spark in her dark blue eyes that had not yet been dulled by grief or fear. Rachel went to help Mrs. Stefa with the dishes.

"Rachel, your plants on the sill here aren't coming on as fast as you hoped. Are you remembering to water them?" Rachel looked sadly at the cuttings, reasonably bushy now, yet with no sign of a bud.

"Yes, but they won't be in flower in time for Mother's birthday, I'm afraid."

"When's that, dear?"

"Two weeks from today. June 24."

"We'll see about that. I'll give you some coal dust from the stove. That'll bring them on, you see." She patted Rachel's dull dark hair and thought how pretty she could have been under other circumstances.

Sabina and Misha were to set out with the baby at about ten-thirty. The Doctor and his contact had thought that the best time to hand her over would be at eleven-thirty. There would still be some activity in the alley then, but the day's smuggling would not be at its busiest, when the children might be in danger of being trampled by rickshaws making their quick getaways. At twelve o'clock a sort of torpor settled on the funny little street for an hour or two, before the afternoon's trading got under way, and at that time they might be too conspicuous.

Korczak himself planned to follow them at a distance in case of any hitches, although in that case there was probably little he would be able to do. He had marked out a precise route for them, and Sabina was to carry Eli's beloved blanket and the canvas bag, leaving Misha to cope with the little girl. The arrangement was that a trough would be lowered once for the baby and, if the coast remained clear, a second time for the few belongings. The Doctor gave Sabina a precious fifty-zloty coin to hand over to Zelig the Paw, a colorful character so nicknamed because he would stand on the corner of Kozla and Franciszkanska and, in his lopsided Polish peasant hat, demand a fee from anyone attempting to enter the alley with a package. If they refused, he would let them have the very rough side of his large "paw." That was something Korczak wanted to spare his little party.

That morning Misha's stomach felt as if it were crawling with live creatures. He was certainly not looking forward to the good-bye with Rachel; the scene at his mother's two days before had been bad enough. Not that it had been tearful or sentimental. In fact, he reflected, as he tried to sip his weak tea while gently warding off Elena's attentions, it had been painful in an unexpected way. His mother had respected their reticence and had not asked a single question. She had been up at the stove heating some water as they all came in. Her face, so thin now with her dark-ringed eyes becoming ever more huge, brightened as it always did when she saw them. Then Misha could see her registering that the day was Monday, that Elena's presence was not scheduled or expected, and that this probably meant that she'd been brought to say good-bye. She had shot an inquiring glance at Misha, who had nodded and said simply, "Wednesday."

But she'd remained calm and proceeded to make tea for the older two, announcing with some satisfaction, "The leaves have only been used once before—quite fresh really!" She let Elena play around, pulling things out of the drawer at the bottom of the big sideboard, her favorite way of spending the time there. Misha saw how their mother struggled to remain composed, saw how she resisted the temptation to smother the child in hugs and kisses. She tried hard now not to touch the children, afraid of infecting them with her illness, but it was a self-imposed rule that she found very hard to keep. Misha found his mother's silent but all-too-evident struggle almost more than he could bear. Mother's last stand, he thought, vaguely remembering something he'd been taught in a history lesson in his old school, in another lifetime.

"I'll just pop next door—see how they are," he had mumbled, leaving Rachel as sole witness for a few minutes. He would have liked to tell the neighbors what was happening, to explain why Mrs. Edelman would probably need extra care and understanding after they'd gone, but he knew he mustn't take even that small risk. Mrs. Stein was very good-hearted, but not discreet.

"I . . . er . . . don't think Mother's too good today. Could you possibly keep an extra eye on her when we've . . . er . . . gone?" he had stammered, feeling rather foolish.

"Of course, Michal. What a shame. We were only saying this morning she seemed a bit more like herself yesterday. That was a nice bit of stew you brought her. . . . You're such a good son."

"Thank you, thank you, good-bye," and Misha just managed to escape being folded in her large and rather smelly bosom. Mrs. Stein had a knack of treating everyone under twenty as if they were five.

Back in the room he had found his mother unwrapping a piece of tissue paper and showing Rachel a small gold locket on a thin neck chain. It was round, with an ornate *L* engraved on the front—*L* for Lili, her first name. She opened it to reveal a miniature portrait of their dead father on the one side, and one of herself on the other.

"I've kept this hidden from you, Misha—I was so afraid you'd insist on exchanging it for food for me." She looked up at Misha and smiled as he came and stood beside her. "I'd always thought it would be yours, Rachel, my love. But if Eli is going away, she might . . . I might . . . well, I've had so little to give her since she was born. . . ." Her face, still dry, was haggard with effort.

"Mother, *darling* Mother, of *course* Eli must have it. After all, I had you, and Father, and Misha, when *I* was two." As she bent to embrace her mother, pressing her face into her shoulder, Rachel was less successful in holding back her tears.

"Perhaps we should go now," said Misha gently, aware that it was up to him to make the first move.

"Yes, yes, of course." Then Mrs. Edelman had knelt down beside her younger daughter, now playing on the floor with an enamel plate and a spoon, and put the necklace around her neck.

"That comes with all my hope and all my love," she said in a hoarse whisper. She kissed her just once on each cheek. Elena whimpered, affected by the solemnity of the moment, and touched the gold chain with a frown of curiosity. Rachel gathered her up, and within seconds it all seemed to be over. With one last superhuman effort, Mrs. Edelman had dragged herself to the doorway and called after them, "Take it off and pin it to her clothes, Rachel. It's dangerous—could just strangle her in her sleep."

"If I didn't know better, I might have thought she was trying to be funny," mumbled Misha, when Rachel had called back a reassurance. And as they went out to meet the Doctor in the hot, smelly street, where the pure cloudless blue mocked them from above, even solemn little Rachel couldn't help a watery smile at this travesty of a joke.

Now that Wednesday had arrived, Misha watched Rachel finish the drying up, knowing very well why she was busying herself so purposefully and wishing that sometimes he could read the members of his family less clearly. He was relieved when she left the room dry-eyed and with no more than a nod in his direction. Elena was by this time on the floor and fighting with Alexander and Adam, a pair of two-year-olds, over a piece of bread one of them had dropped.

A few minutes later, when Mrs. Stefa summoned them to check Elena's things, Rachel reappeared with the gold locket in a tiny package tied, together with a scroll of paper, by a smart blue ribbon. Misha thought he recognized the ribbon as the one Rachel had been wearing when they first entered the orphanage over a year ago. That was before they'd had their heads shaved, of course, a precaution against lice that the Doctor had always insisted on with newly arrived children, even in the old days before the ghetto. He would make it fun for them by clipping shapes or initials onto their scalps. He was right, too; there were probably fewer lice per head in the Orphans' Home than in any other house within the ghetto wall.

"Will you put this in for me, Mrs. Stefa? It's the story of the beginning of her life. I thought that one day she would want to know, and in case we're not . . . well, anyway, this way she'll have it, won't she?" She stood erect, her expressive features for once quite still, and Misha, watching her carefully, understood that she was attempting to follow their mother's example. Mrs. Stefa, herself wearier than any of them could have known, was overcome.

"That's the best present you could have given her, pet," she said, making no attempt to disguise a choke. "And you write so nicely."

Rachel shrugged. "Well, it's all I can do. Please, may I say good-bye now?" Elena was sitting against the end of the crib, sucking her thumb and looking tired after the early morning exertions. Rachel bent over and kissed the top of her sister's head. The baby barely looked up. Afterward Rachel told Misha that those few moments had seemed to pass in endlessly slow motion. "Like the day they took Father away to bury him." And that was all. Misha guessed she'd go upstairs and do her best to find a quiet corner where she could sit and write in her diary. He knew very well that she'd need to be left alone.

It was only at that moment that he realized he himself had

nothing to give as a farewell present. Nothing at all. The only remotely valuable things he had left were his father's wallet and belts, and he dared not part with them, in case he should need them for his mother. It gave him an unpleasant feeling of panic, all the same, like the dream he had once had in which he'd arrived to take an important exam at school and then realized he'd done no reviewing for it at all.

When they left, it was by the kitchen door, quietly and unobtrusively, for the Doctor had wanted as few people as possible to know about their departure. Above them, at the entrance to the courtyard, the orphanage flag fluttered bright in the sunshine. Doctor Korczak had put a lot of thought into that flag, and his Aryan friend, Hanna Olczak, who would one day write the story of his life, had helped him to design it, back in 1940. On one side, on a green background, were the chestnut flowers—for Korczak a symbol of perpetual blossoming—and on the other, against a white background, the blue Star of David, symbol of a persecuted people.

It was to be a long walk, from one end of the ghetto to the other. Because of the deep indentation of Aryan territory, they couldn't take a direct route but had to strike west from Sienna Street and up over the Chlodna Street footbridge before eventually being able to bear east down Leszno Street. Misha was very familiar with the route as far as his mother's room, but they had at least twice that distance to cover. Misha was soon tired with the extra weight of the baby, and their stops grew more and more frequent. Elena could walk short distances at a time, but that made their progress agonizingly slow, and, in any case, she much preferred to be carried. Twice, before they could stop her, she sat down in protest on the filthy pavement, her hands outstretched in appeal, and even today Misha couldn't help being irritated. To begin with, Sabina tried to chat to make Misha feel more at ease, but soon she, too, needed all her breath. To get anywhere in those rubbish-filled, overcrowded streets required precious energy, and it always seemed to Misha as if the main tide of movement was against, rather than with him. It was also important not to touch anyone, if it could possibly be avoided, for fear of contracting typhus.

They passed several soup stands, one of which was selling some delicious-smelling sausages.

"Soggidge, soggidge," chanted Elena, as she recognized the smell. She began to cry. Misha put her down and wiped his brow, wishing it weren't so hot.

"I suppose we could . . ." Sabina was really thinking aloud, feeling the fifty zlotys in her pocket.

"Top-quality sausage," shouted the vendor, a tall fierce-looking man with a cap pulled down almost to his eyes. "Forty zlotys—unbeatable value!"

Sabina and Misha looked at each other, relieved to be spared further temptation. The price was ridiculous. They walked on, Elena still whimpering at the thought of sausage.

Near the Catholic church, recently walled off so as to place it beyond the ghetto boundary, they found a low wall set back a little way from the main thoroughfare. There was even a worn patch of grass beside it, probably left by mistake when the workmen had sealed off the churchyard. They stopped to rest on the wall, depositing Elena on the cleanest bit of grass. Misha was surprised to hear from Sabina how, when the church was still on ghetto territory, five of the other children had written to its priest asking for permission to play in the churchyard early on Saturday mornings. Sabina remembered some of their wording, so touched had she been by it: "We long for a little fresh air and the sight of green things. Our place is cramped and airless. We would like to have some contact with nature." The Doctor had agreed to let them hand over the request in person, so Miss Esterka had escorted them as far as the church. When they arrived, the priest, with his congregation of Jews who'd been converted to Christianity, was saying Mass. While they waited, they heard the approach of an SS patrol along the street, so they had pried open the heavy door and slipped inside to hide. It was the first time any of them had been inside a church. They were awed by its size and rich ornaments and stayed huddled together just inside the door. After Mass the priest had come up to them and told them kindly that they could play in the churchyard, as long as they were quiet. But he had warned them that soon the church would no longer be included in the ghetto and that he would probably be taken away. His prediction had come true within a week, and Sami and Abrasha and their three friends had had just one playtime on the grass among the graves.

It was just as well that Misha and Sabina could not see through the new wall, for they would have been confronted with a desolate scene. On the other side broken stone crucifixes littered the rough ground, and dozens of pews and other items of church furniture lay in haphazard piles, fractured and useless now, as the building was being systematically stripped, like so many synagogues and other churches before it, for conversion to an armaments warehouse. The Nazis had little use for places of worship. Neither could Misha and Sabina know that the priest and many of his parishioners had already been "resettled in the East," though this was a phrase with which they were to become all too familiar in the coming weeks.

They watched Elena as she spread the palms of her hands over the strange gray-green stuff; then she bent down, her little bottom sticking up in the air, and rubbed her cheek against it.

"No, no, Eli, you'll get filthy and you must stay nice and clean for . . ." Misha broke off and looked at Sabina. For what? For whom? That was the big question in both their minds.

"We'd better get going again now," he went on instead. "We mustn't keep Mister Doctor waiting." Doctor Korczak planned to wait some way down Franciszkanska Street from the entrance to Kozla Alley to make sure that they had got that far safely.

"No. Poor man—he has more haggling to do at the Supply

Authority first. About some potatoes, Mrs. Stefa said. She says he finds the begging the hardest thing of all, though he never complains about it."

"He looks so ill these days. And I don't think he sleeps more than two or three hours a night, you know." They were both silent, thinking of the man they both loved and depended upon so much, and yet of whom they knew strangely little. As he scooped Elena off the ground and dusted her down, Misha went on: "Yet he takes so much trouble over each one of us, he makes you feel you're the only person he cares about. Look at all the effort he must have put into this plan for Eli, and she's just one in two hundred."

"He doesn't give anything away about himself, though, does he?" said Sabina. She pictured in her mind the Doctor's red-bearded face and the sad, rather crooked smile. "I mean, you can see him making an effort to laugh and be cheerful, but there's that sorrow in his face all the time."

"Well, that's hardly surprising," said Misha almost impatiently. It annoyed him when people stated the obvious, as his friend Viktor often did.

"Maybe not. But there's something mysterious about him, all the same," she said firmly. "Come on, let's get going." She tucked Elena's bag carefully under her arm, as she eyed a group of ragged little boys peering at them from a few feet away. From now on even snatches of conversation became impossible as they wove and darted their way through the tattered crowds. But they were eventually able to check the time by the clock in Gesia Street and found they were actually ahead of schedule. They slowed down, Misha aware of his thumping heart.

"Well, little girl," he said, changing Elena to his other side for the hundredth time. It was a matter of pride with him not to take Sabina up on her several offers to help carry the baby. "I'd never have thought to complain that you were too heavy!"

At eleven-fifteen they caught sight of Doctor Korczak standing outside the Supply Authority. He gave them their thumbs up sign, the cue to move up toward the junction of Kozla Alley and Franciszkanska Street. The Doctor had warned them in their briefing session the previous evening not to behave furtively, as if they had something to hide, but they now realized that that was easier said than done. Misha busied himself with wiping Elena's nose, a job he'd always found distasteful. As they turned the corner, unobtrusively, they hoped, Sabina felt the dreaded tap on her shoulder. She jumped and gave a little exclamation.

"Stop!" hissed a voice. "Don't be shy, auntie, hand over fifty for a package fee." He looked pointedly at Elena's little piece of luggage, tucked under Sabina's arm.

"Oh, oh, yes," Sabina stuttered, delving into her pocket. Thank goodness we were warned, she thought, with heartfelt relief. Zelig the Paw was a rough, eccentric man, who had knocked out more than one unsuspecting fee refuser. But he had one weakness, and that was for small children. Now he put out one large red paw to pat Elena on the head; Misha darted out of his reach, unsure as to his intentions, and the startled baby began to cry. Zelig, offended, muttered some swearwords and shouted at them to be off, so that the little party walked on into the alley feeling more conspicuous than ever and hardly daring to look to the left or right.

However, after a few minutes of mingling with the throng—more purposeful and businesslike than on other ghetto streets—they began to feel less exposed. For Misha, whose own smuggling had been confined to secret holes in the cemetery wall, it was an amazing scene. Small tables stood outside every house, loaded with fruit, vegetables, and sacks of rye, millet, and barley. Each stand and cart was surrounded by people, most of them, Misha realized as he became more accustomed to the sight, looking on longingly rather than buying. He did see one or two women buy potatoes and carrots in pathetically small quantities, and he saw plenty of "porters" or "strollers," hurrying down the street with sacks of flour and groats on their backs, anxious to pass on their incriminating loads before the Gestapo should catch them.

Presently Misha noticed that all the even-numbered non-Jewish houses, whose front entrances gave onto the other side, had their back windows secured from top to bottom by wire mesh. He also noticed that small wooden troughs had been inserted lengthwise between the bars at two or three ground floor windows. At the bottom of one of these troughs a tall broad-shouldered porter with a sack was waiting. Misha stopped to watch, fascinated. Soon, and with no obvious warning, a load of rye came thudding down the trough in a flurry of dust and, scarcely before Misha had had time to register what was happening, it disappeared into the waiting sack and was hoisted onto two giant shoulders. At the bottom of the neighboring trough was a knot of people of different ages, all apparently insulting each other in colorful language.

Their destination was an even-numbered house at the far end of the alley. It looked very closed up and deserted, decidedly unpromising. The only good thing about it, Misha realized, was that, unlike most of the other houses on the same side, it didn't seem to have attracted any hangers-on. It hadn't occurred to him before how awkward it might be to hoist Elena up on the first leg of her journey, in full view of a possibly curious and even hostile audience. The Doctor had certainly made light of this. He had felt sure that no Jewish smuggler would sabotage an attempt to rescue a Jewish child, and, in any case, there could be no question of the transfer taking place at night. It would have been far too dangerous to attempt it after curfew. "Not that the alley itself is much quieter at night," he had added. But despite the Doctor's optimism, Misha looked doubtfully at the back of this house that was to be his sister's route to freedom. He wished that the ground floor windows weren't so firmly barred, for it would have been a good deal easier to pass her through at that level, rather than at the first floor.

Sabina and Misha stood watching the house from the other side of the alley, once again feeling very conspicuous. Without realizing it, they had begun exchanging words in a whisper; Elena, tired by the walk and the crowds and the heat, rubbed her eyes as wisps of fair hair stuck damply to her brow. Misha held her more tightly, suddenly intensely aware of the great unknown into which he was about to pass this little replica of their father. As if trying to drill a message into her head from his own, he laid his cheek hard against her temple and offered a silent but insistent little apology for all the things he hadn't done or felt for her in the past eighteen months.

"I've felt I hated you at times, but I don't really. I don't really. I'm sorry. I'm sorry." Those ineffectual words again.

Then, suddenly, a hand appeared at the first floor window, and an area of about half a square meter of wire mesh—presumably precut—was removed. A wooden tray with a lip approximately ten centimeters high was lowered on two ropes: In the tray were two white paper bags of flour each tied with a red string, the signal they had been told to expect. Misha looked around him guiltily as he and Sabina darted forward, and, sure enough, the appearance of the tray had attracted attention. Two teenage girls in headscarves came forward and grabbed the unexpected loot, pausing only for a second to gape with surprise at Sabina and Misha, who stood mesmerized and were clearly not going to make any attempt to fight over the prize. But within moments Misha had pulled himself together. He stooped, placed Elena on the tray, bent to kiss her, and at the same time tugged three times on the rope.

"Quick, Sabina—her bag, *now*."

"No, that's for—"

"Now!" Misha knew intuitively that the bag must go with his

sister this time. It was contrary to instruction—the Doctor hadn't been sure how much room there'd be—but when it came to the crucial moment, Misha couldn't let her be separated from her few precious belongings. He seized the bag and threw it onto the tray just as it started to rise.

Elena, now really frightened, tried to heave herself up. "Eeca, Eeca," she cried, holding one side of the tray with both hands and twisting herself around so as to appeal down at him.

"*Please,* God, don't let her tip over. Let her make it to the window," Misha prayed. He hadn't appreciated how easy it might be for her to fall, and as he watched her go, his heart seemed to be beating right up in his throat. Then he saw two arms pull the tray inside and thought he caught a glimpse of long fair hair leaning over, but the windows were grimy and opaque and his eyes could have deceived him. As the hand, probably a woman's, reached out to fit the wire square back into place, he heard a shriek of fear from his sister and then—nothing.

The very next moment something extremely strange happened. A hiss of "*Passover*" came down the alley, relaying itself from group to group like wind in grass. Literally within seconds the funny little street was transformed. Open doorways were slammed shut, loaded tables disappeared, ropes were hoisted out of sight. People who moments before had been arguing and bargaining stood nonchalantly back against house walls, as if enjoying a relaxing chat. Sabina and Misha stood in a doorway across the street from "their" house. There was no sign of life; they both strained eager eyes, but the grubby, wired-up and, in one or two places, cracked windowpanes gave nothing away.

"Thank *goodness* you threw the bag up in time."

"Yes, I knew—somehow. She just *had* to take something of us with her."

They waited. They thought they heard people moan the dreaded word "Gestapo," but after five endless minutes nothing had happened. No black uniforms appeared, no shouts, no shots, no boots marching to that familiar devil rhythm. Perhaps it had been a false alarm. But false or not, they waited for what must have been nearly an hour. Even though there was nothing incriminating about them now, the last thing they wanted was to run into an SS patrol. And the tray did not reappear.

Eventually they made their way back along the alley, now dozing in its period of midday rest. It was amazing, thought Misha, that their transaction hadn't attracted more attention, but it had all happened so fast—at real smuggler speed. The Doctor was waiting anxiously for them outside the Supply Authority. He said nothing, scanning their faces keenly for news of the outcome. He linked arms with them for reassurance—his own, as always, conspicuously free of the yellow arm band—but they soon had to give up walking three abreast because progress was too slow. In narrow Karmelicka Street they were forced into single file, though they managed to keep very close together. Scarcely a day went by when someone wasn't mown down by a Nazi car careering at full speed along that teeming thoroughfare. Their favored targets were the rickshaws, the two-seater foot-propelled tricycles that were the ghetto's only means of wheeled transport. Sometimes, not content with running down their victims, the drivers would get out and wield at random their clubs and rifle butts. And unfortunately Karmelicka was a necessary hazard to be negotiated because it was the only street connecting the main ghetto with the Little Ghetto, in which the orphanage was situated.

At last, as they turned into Sliska Street and the orphanage came into sight on the corner, the Doctor felt able to ask, "So—how did it go?"

Misha told him, and then blurted out—though strangely it wasn't something he'd been thinking about on the return journey—"I seem to be the only person who didn't give her anything."

The Doctor stopped in his tracks and made the boy do the

same by holding his arm. He turned to look at him. "Only a second chance, Misha. Not a bad present for a little Jewish girl these days." He spoke slowly and seriously, despite the understatement: He always tried not to share his fears and misgivings with the children, and in recent weeks he had already said more to Misha than he would have wished. Now, for the first time, Misha was aware that he had done something really very special.

CHAPTER 11

MISHA AND RACHEL HAD no time to brood about Eli, for the very next day the Doctor broke a second piece of news to them. He had for some time been worried about Misha's daily trips to see his mother; although many of the children had at least one relative living nearby, Misha was the only one who was old enough to feel responsible for maintaining a close surviving member of the family. There were so many dangers on the streets now, and since the Night of Blood in April the situation had been worsening steadily, with the Nazis committing murder daily and indiscriminately. Any Jewish life, or so it seemed, could be snuffed out on the whim of a moment. On May 29, nine hundred men, women, and children had been rounded up and sent out of the ghetto to an undisclosed destination. Those early days of widespread death by starvation and disease had been desolate enough, but in his heart the Doctor knew that, despite his brave words in young ears, there was worse—and much worse—to come.

So when he heard that the elderly mother-in-law of one of his friends and former patients, now living with the rest of his family in Panska Street, had died, leaving a vacant bed in the flat, he was quick to ask the favor. Could Mrs. Edelman move in? He, somehow, would undertake to see she did not become a financial burden on the family when her money ran out, as he knew it must soon do even though the proceeds from her furniture, which she couldn't take with her, would help for a little while. The Bauer family owed the Doctor at least one favor; in 1940 he had, or so they believed, saved their small son from death by typhus by bringing down his fever at the crucial moment, and they readily agreed to receive the new tenant, sick though she was.

"Panska will be much safer—it's only around the corner and there's less activity down here in the Little Ghetto, anyway." The smile of relief on Misha's face was ample reward for Korczak's initiative. But then it disappeared as quickly as it had come.

"What's the matter?"

"How will we get her there? She's too weak to walk."

"We'll transport her in style. She shall travel in the Orphans' Home's own private rickshaw."

"Rickshaw! I thought you didn't approve of them because they're such hard work for the pedaler."

"I don't. Not when small children are made to drive them for adult passengers, and at a pittance. But there are exceptions, Misha, to every rule. And Sami and Staszek are making a rickshaw—it's their own idea. They thought it might be helpful for bringing back supplies sometimes."

"I see," Misha's doubt was plain.

"They've nearly finished. One or two more days—I've been promised some more old cycle parts for this very afternoon."

"Will it be safe?"

"You shall ride in it first to test it. Don't be so mistrustful. Stash is first-rate with his hands, and Sami's an enthusiastic helper."

"Mmm."

"And, Misha, I think it would be nice if we invited Stash to drive when we collect your mother, don't you?"

"Yes, yes, of course." Be nice. Stash needs encouragement. He's so unsure of himself, so modest, Misha told himself quickly, trying, without much success, to hide his disappointment. But the Doctor saw and thought he understood.

"Just let him play his part, that's all I ask."

"Of course he must." Misha was ashamed, again. What *had* happened to the even temper and kind nature his parents had always attributed to him? Did one, perhaps, need a full stomach in order to think unselfish thoughts?

The day they moved Mrs. Edelman to Panska Street was the day on which a hundred and ten Jews in the ghetto prison were executed, in retaliation for the "disobedience" of other Jews to the instructions of the Nazi police. Stash drove the Doctor and Misha to the building in Orla Street and carried the one suitcase containing what was left of Mrs. Edelman's belongings down the two narrow flights of stairs, taking care not to step on the various people camped on the landings. Misha started to lift his mother out of bed; she had dressed herself already and was leaning back against the pillows, tired out by the exertion.

"No, Misha, my love, this time I'll walk out of the building." She pushed herself up into a standing position and made her way cautiously to the doorway. Progress down the stairs was slow, with frequent pauses for breath. On the first landing an old man had fallen asleep and, oblivious to everything around him, was barring their way, so Misha picked his mother up and deposited her gently on his other side. But, as she had determined, Mrs. Edelman did leave the house on her own two feet, and even found the energy to embrace Mrs. Stein and her little girl, who came down to the street to wave an emotional farewell.

"Take care, Lili. I hope you'll let us come and see you."

"You've been so kind, Ruth. May God reward you." Mrs. Edelman kissed her neighbor, and Misha, looking on, winced at the difference in their sizes: his mother, so frail you could almost make out each individual bone beneath the bluish white flesh, and Mrs. Stein, still surprisingly well preserved and robust to look at, despite the years of deprivation. Misha made no attempt to take over the saddle from Stash, but helped his mother onto the passenger seat and settled himself down beside her. The Doctor deposited the armful of Mrs. Edelman's bedding onto Misha's lap, then stooped and stroked the head of Mrs. Stein's black-haired daughter.

"I bet you're a mischievous one." He smiled.

Her mother grasped his arm, looked intently into his cracked, thick-lensed glasses, and whispered urgently, "What's going to happen to us, Mister Doctor? What's going to happen? Do you think it's true what everyone keeps saying? That we're all going to be taken away? They're talking about tens of thousands having to be evacuated; they say there's a quarter of a million Nazi soldiers marching on Warsaw to take over our homes because theirs have been bombed; they say—" Poor Mrs. Stein could scarcely stop the momentum when Korczak interrupted her. He felt her panic clutch at him, threatening to tear the vestment of calm that, in the orphanage, he strove so hard to preserve.

"Mrs. Stein, I know what they're saying. But no one really knows what's in store for us. We must hope, and go on hoping, and above all go on trying to survive, for the sake of these little ones." He bent his aching back to pat the child's head once again, but as he straightened up and extricated himself from her grasp he felt a rush of dizziness in his own head.

Mrs. Stein stood for a while looking after the little party, shaking her head in fear and bewilderment. She was going to miss Lili Edelman; having her to worry and fuss over had helped her to keep her mind on everyday matters.

Meanwhile, the travelers on the rickshaw had had an unpleasant shock. They were just about to turn into Leszno Street when shouts and a squeal of brakes rang out. Misha shut his eyes and instinctively turned his head into his mother's shoulder. She did not avert her own face but shielded his with one hand, for she did not want him to see what she had seen. Another rickshaw just ahead of them had been mown down by an armored car occupied by four SS men in their bright black uniforms. The unfortunate vehicle lay on its side, crushed and beyond repair. Its driver, a young man, was pinned to the ground, his leg trapped by the twisted metal; he looked up aghast, as one of the officers approached him, slowly and menacingly, his pistol drawn and ready. The two women and a small boy who had been riding in the back of the rickshaw crouched at the side, huddled together, the child screaming. Stash, usually rather slow in his reactions, took no more than a few seconds to sum up the situation. Jumping off the saddle, he ran to the back of their own rickshaw, seized the rear axle, and dragged the makeshift vehicle back into Orla Street with several giant, fear-propelled strides. In two more seconds, Misha had pulled himself together and jumped out to help him. When the Doctor caught up with them, breathless and flustered after running up on his noisy, wood-soled shoes, he needed only a quick glance at their faces to guess more or less what had happened. Two pistol shots rang out, confirming his suspicions.

They waited quietly for about five minutes, until they saw the armored car resume its journey and pass the end of the street, before resuming theirs. Now Misha insisted that the Doctor ride with his mother—at least as far as the Chlodna Street footbridge where he would have to get out to help them up the steps— while he pushed from behind to make Stash's job easier. As they passed the scene of slaughter, he turned away his head.

By the time they arrived in Panska Street, Mrs. Edelman was very tired indeed. It would have been easier to carry her up the three flights of stairs, but she insisted on trying to haul herself up, one or two steps at a time, and neither Misha nor the Doctor liked to deprive her of this remnant of independence. It was particularly difficult because, since the banisters had long ago been removed for firewood, she had only the wall for support.

Leon Bauer welcomed them very politely, formally even, and insisted that Misha and Stash and the Doctor stay for a cup of weak tea. He told Mrs. Edelman that it was an honor to have her share the humble accommodations with his family, and apologized profusely that she would have to share her room with his wife's aunt. He looked embarrassed at this point and mentioned that the old lady had become a little weak-minded as a result of her suffering.

Misha certainly did not much like the look of Leon Bauer's relative. A woman of about sixty, she did not acknowledge them but just stared absently ahead of her as she constantly curled and recurled a lock of hair around her index finger.

He felt quite homesick for friendly, gossipy Mrs. Stein and was relieved when Leon produced quite a handsome screen, which would give his mother at least a measure of privacy. Misha quickly made up the bed while she waited in the kitchen next door; Leon had also managed somehow to make a little table and a chest of drawers available, so Misha arranged one or two photos and his mother's favorite books on these, to give her corner of the room a personal touch.

After the tea Misha helped her into bed and waited until a coughing fit had subsided and she'd almost fallen asleep. On the short way back to the orphanage Misha insisted that he should give Stash a ride in the back of his own rickshaw; as they put it away in an outhouse in the corner of the courtyard, Misha said, "You were great, Stash—I'm really grateful." He watched the broad, fair-complexioned face suffuse with a blush of pleasure, and was glad.

When, some days later, Rachel woke up on the morning of her mother's birthday, she felt a pleasant flutter of anticipation in her stomach, such as she had almost forgotten existed. Her care and attention had paid off, and the day before one of the geranium plants had opened most of its first flower. The Doctor had promised she could have one of the blooms from his own carefully tended window box if hers didn't open in time, but that wouldn't have been the same.

Misha, too, had been busy preparing for the day. Like Rachel he had a moderate talent for drawing, which both his parents had always encouraged, and he'd produced pen sketches of Rachel and Elena (the latter, before her escape, when she was unwell and so sat still long enough to be sketched). He'd asked Sami to make a frame, in exchange for an old pair of shoes that Sami had always admired. He felt rather guilty about the deal, knowing that the orphanage store needed shoes that were still wearable, and that these were still too big for Sami. But he badly wanted to give his mother a present, this of all years. At thirteen his faith in miracles had all but disappeared. Sami had produced a smooth, rounded frame out of an old piece of plank, which he had then stained and polished.

In a moment of inspiration Misha invited Sami to a little birthday celebration, and Viktor, too. He would have liked to ask Stash as well, in appreciation of the part he had played in the move, but knew that Rachel would want Genia to be there and felt that it might be unfair to take too many people to Mr. Bauer's flat. The extra company would be exhausting for his mother, he knew, and they would have to be brief, but he hoped they could make a party of the occasion. The Doctor thought it was a marvelous idea and even found time, the day before, to call at Panska Street on his morning forage for food, and arrange with Leon Bauer to move his aunt out of the room for an hour or so the next afternoon. It was extraordinary, thought Leon Bauer, as he escorted the Doctor down the steep, cluttered stairway, how the burden of responsibilities that weighed down on him—even more so now, since he had been forced to assume control of the badly run Children's Refuge on Dzielna Street as well—never seemed to lessen his concern for the intimate details of his children's lives.

Rachel, delighted at her brother's suggestion, invited Genia to join them for the celebration in Panska Street. When they all set off, Misha carried the basket of goodies: maize cakes, a pot of synthetic honey, six slices of Mrs. Stefa's special carrot cake, and a tiny packet of the Doctor's own personal coffee grounds.

These were smuggled over to him specially by a family of well-wishers on the other side, who always added some fresh beans to the grounds. He accepted them gratefully, for they helped him keep awake during the quiet small hours of the morning when he could write his memoirs and think, and just savor the silence. Rachel was holding her plants, a pot crooked in each arm, and Genia, for some reason, carried Misha's package.

Barely had they turned into short Komitet Street when they were accosted by a "snatcher," a ragged boy of about ten or eleven, filthy and barefoot, his upper clothes tied together by bits of string. On an impulse he grabbed the package from Genia with his two thin arms and ran down the street, back in the direction from which they had come, before Genia really understood what was happening. She let out a wail; Misha pushed the basket of food at Viktor and yelled, "Sami, after him. He's got my pictures!" They raced down the street to the corner, where Misha caught a glimpse of the culprit disappearing into a crowd of people around a soup stand. He thought he saw him reemerge: "Come on, Sami!" But Sami needed no urging. Misha had not run so fast for a very long time, and his breath seemed to scrape his throat as it tore from his chest with the exertion, but his feet carried him on. The boy had snatched his mother's precious birthday present—he had nothing else to give her, as he had had nothing to give Elena. These twin thoughts throbbed inside him as he pounded down Sliska Street, darting between knots of people, knocking into others who weren't quick enough to get out of the way, even shoving at a mother begging with a baby carriage. The fear of physical contact with its risk of typhus was far from his mind at that moment.

"Thief, thief," he gasped out, not caring what people might think of him. But no one took any notice; snatchers were as much an everyday part of the ghetto as food lines and crowds and filth and dead bodies covered in newspaper.

By the time they reached the junction with Twarda Street, they knew they had lost him; it was a busy main thoroughfare, and he could have taken refuge anywhere. Besides that, two armored cars were approaching from the right, and Sami, remembering what had nearly happened to Stash and Misha in the rickshaw, took hold of the elder boy's shirt and pulled him back. Misha was beyond tears. He stood back against a wall, suddenly limp, and he quite literally retched from rage and bitter, bitter disappointment.

Sami put a hand on his shoulder and said shyly, "Just think, Michal, he's going to get one hell of a shock when he sees what he's got for dinner—two little girls and an old piece of wood!"

"And I hope they *choke* him—slowly," Misha managed to hiss murderously between clenched teeth.

"Come on, we must get back to the others now." Misha let Sami, sensible beyond his nine years, guide him back down the street, glad of the little arm through his own. He felt giddy and sick.

The others knew as soon as they came back into sight that the package had not been retrieved. Rachel looked anxiously at her brother's distraught white face, but said nothing at first. They carried on in silence, but when they reached the door of the tall tenement building in Panska Street, Rachel held out one of the geraniums: "You give her one of these, Misha."

He was touched and, as on the Night of Blood, when his tears had been summoned not by impotent rage but by the report of a kind gesture, he felt the familiar stinging at the back of his eyes. But he wasn't ready for the offer, and he refused it roughly.

"No, no, they're yours. Hardly the same, is it?"

Rachel nodded in understanding, remembering how she had felt about the Doctor's offer of flowers that had bloomed before her own.

"Come on, then," she coaxed. "Mother will understand."

Genia looked on, fascinated by a side of Misha she had never seen before, and not sure whether or not to feel guilty. "I'm so sorry, Misha."

He glared at her. "Not your fault," he growled, with huge effort and no grace.

Lili Edelman had spent the morning trying to sleep in order to be fresh for the party. She was sitting up in bed when they came in, having rubbed the last of her rouge into her hollow cheeks and combed her hair with special care so as to hide the thinning area in the front. She held out her arms with a smile of pleasure. "How lovely to see you all." She looked eagerly for Misha, but he wasn't there; he couldn't bear to watch Rachel offer her present, so he had hung behind.

"Go on, I'll only spoil it for you," he said, as he pushed his sister roughly through the door.

"They're *beautiful*. My favorite color. It's so—alive. You clever, clever girl, Rachel." Mrs. Edelman patted her daughter's head with pride. "Put them on the windowsill—they like the light, and I can see them best there. What a wonderful surprise."

Misha, listening from the other side of the door, scrunched his features together, willing her to stop. When she did, he made his entry. "Happy birthday, Mother." He bent to kiss her. "I—I haven't anything for you. I. . . ," and the rest of the words simply stuck in his throat.

"Mama, he drew you two fantastic pictures. Well, one of them wasn't 'cause it was of me, but . . ." And Rachel went on to tell her of all the trouble he and Sami had gone to, and then about the disaster that had struck in Komitet Street. Misha, awkward and still, holding one of his mother's hands, was grateful to his sister for supplying the words. Viktor and Sami, meanwhile, busied themselves putting the food on the table, while Genia, feeling embarrassed, wandered over to the grimy window to inspect the view. There was a knock at the door, and Leon put his head around, offering dishes and boiling water. Perhaps, thought Misha, the occasion might not be completely ruined after all.

"You know, darling," said Mrs. Edelman, whose clear, pleasant-toned voice had not been impaired by illness and hunger, "they always do say that it's the thought, not the gift, that counts. And for the first time I can really appreciate what that means. I would have treasured those pictures, but it was a lovely, lovely thought, and I can still treasure that. I'm so touched that you went to all that trouble. And you, too, Samek. *Thank* you." The episode had given her the chance to comfort and reassure her son, a luxury she had long been deprived of, and curiously there was a look of something like contentment on her face.

Rachel then added, "And, Mish, I couldn't say this to you down there, but you can't blame that kid. You don't know how many mouths he has to feed, or . . ."

Misha didn't reply. He was feeling a bit better, but not nearly in a mood to forgive. Sometimes he wished his earnest little sister wasn't so damned *nice*.

It was, of course, customary for the person whose birthday was being celebrated to make a wish. The children didn't like to remind Mrs. Edelman, for it would have been somehow cruel, and might have destroyed the atmosphere they'd created, which was happy in the way in which an oasis can be beautiful. But Mrs. Edelman was not going to be done out of her birthday wish.

"Listen, all of you," she said, just before they attacked the carrot cake. "I have a special wish today. It is—it is that one day you may all have the chance to live as children should live." Then she gave them the traditional Jewish toast "L'chayim"—"to life"—and to that they all lifted their cups of weak coffee, for never had any toast seemed so appropriate.

CHAPTER 12

WHEN HE WAS SMALLER, the arrival of his mother's birthday had made Misha begin to think with anticipation of his own, six weeks later. But this year the thought that his fourteenth birthday was fast approaching was not welcome. For fourteen was the age when, traditionally, Korczak's children would leave the orphanage to go on to jobs or apprenticeships. Conditions in the ghetto were so hard now that the Doctor couldn't bring himself to turn anyone out, but Misha was all too aware that if he stayed on he would be taking up a place in the relative security of the Orphans' Home that was badly needed by any number of younger children less able to fend for themselves.

But *where* could he go? There was no one in the family left in Warsaw, and, though the Edelmans had had plenty of friends and acquaintances, they would all be doing their best for the remnants of their own families. There was no one Misha felt he could ask even for a corner of a floor to sleep on. His father had had a younger sister, married to a pharmacist with two little boys, but they had managed to obtain false papers soon after the ghetto had been sealed off. Misha thought of his plump, pretty aunt with a pang of regret; he wondered if he'd ever see her and taste her special apple cake again. There was nice Aunt Anna, too, his father's first cousin, but he knew that her husband had been deported to work in an armaments factory in Germany, and she and the children had fled to the south of Poland, where her family had a farm. There was, of course, his uncle, his father's younger brother, but he was very much the black sheep of the family, having become a member of the Jewish police. Misha didn't like to dwell on the memory of Uncle Marc. And Mrs. Edelman had been an only child, and her parents had both died between the wars.

Misha continued to visit his mother every day in the rundown tenement building on Panska Street, and Rachel nearly always came with him now that she was so much closer. The worry of his approaching independence was almost constantly on his mind, but he dared not share it with either his mother or sister. Mrs. Edelman's supply of money was dwindling fast. Leon and Mister Doctor had got less than they had hoped for the furniture in the old flat, and the nice old sideboard, fated to be used as firewood, had fetched the equivalent of three kilos of flour and some powdered eggs. Misha's smuggling escapades, regular monthly affairs up until the Night of Blood, had now had to stop with only about six hundred zlotys left. With bread at around thirty-five zlotys a loaf, that was not a comfortable sum. Although she actually ate very little, Misha knew that she was getting outstanding value for money at Leon Bauer's, where she was sharing the family rations for a hundred zlotys a week. But he had to pretend he hadn't noticed, for he knew that she couldn't possibly afford to pay more. He knew it was important for her to feel she was paying her way, so he made a point of never mentioning the subject.

He began to get to know and like Leon. He was a quiet, shy young man, very careful and fastidious about the apartment and his own appearance, and unexpectedly witty in a dry way. Misha suspected that his wife had been mentally affected by the rigors of ghetto life, for she always seemed to be either at the height of hilarity or sitting silent and self-obsessed in a corner of the kitchen. Misha felt sorry for Leon, having responsibility for two such unappealing female relatives. His young son, Aronek, the one the Doctor had saved from typhus, spent most of his time with a little girl down on the floor below. After a while (on the days when Rachel was collected by the Doctor or someone else from the Orphans' Home) Leon took to waylaying Misha as he was leaving after his visit and offering him tea or even watery cabbage soup, which was the household's staple daily diet.

Increasingly on the days when Misha was invited for tea, there would be other young men there as well. They were actually only eighteen or nineteen, but to Misha they were young men. One of them, Joseph, had the saddest, most beautiful dark eyes Misha had ever seen. With his shock of black curly hair and broken nose he cut a romantic figure, and his conversation was in keeping with that image. They would talk of smuggling in guns and other arms, of building hideouts behind false doors and in cellars, of getting the different political underground groups in the ghetto into one big organization, strong enough to fight the Nazis. It was heady stuff for a boy whose main preoccupation over the past twenty months had been food. Suddenly, it seemed, there might be more to the future than mere survival. They talked about people and ideas he had never heard or thought of, but, curiously, they didn't seem bothered by his presence. He listened, enthralled, and felt proud and pleased just to be there. When, at Leon's suggestion, sad-eyed Joseph took Misha's father's wallet and promised to bring him the money in two days, he had perfect trust in the young man, whose second name he didn't even know.

It was Leon who came for Misha and Rachel the morning Lili Edelman fell into a coma. A few words with the Doctor, who came pattering down the stairs in his green apron, a worried frown making the little furrows above his nose more noticeable than ever, ensured that Rachel was instantly relieved from clearing-up duty and Misha was called out of his Hebrew lesson. They knew immediately what was happening. Misha unashamedly took Rachel's proffered hand as they half ran with Leon back to Panska Street.

Misha leaned over his mother, whose face had gone a strange greenish color. He felt as if his own blood were draining completely away from the upper half of his body; suddenly he was light-headed and heavy-legged. An unpleasant rasping sound was coming from her throat. He took one cold hand, Rachel the other.

Rachel whispered, "Mother, it's Rachel and Misha. If you can hear me, just press my hand. Press my hand, Mother, please. Press my hand."

But there was no answering pressure, and Rachel knew, before Misha, that their mother was already beyond their reach. Misha made toward the door in some wild hope that the Doctor, who had hurried on after them, would be able to do something. But the Doctor just stood there, shaking his head sadly, and when Misha turned back toward the bed, the painful rattling sound had stopped altogether.

Thanks to the Doctor's contacts and the money obtained by Joseph for their father's wallet—all of which went for bribing guards, to allow the little party into the cemetery—Rachel and Misha were able to see their mother given an almost-decent burial. At least her last resting place was not in a mass grave, and, in the tiny space found for her, Rachel was allowed to plant her two geraniums. Misha, as the eldest surviving male relative, was allowed to intone the prayer for the departed. He did so without a tremor in his voice, and the thing inside him was strangely still; after all, could there be anything much worse to come now?

Leon attended the funeral, and it was on the way back to the Little Ghetto that he said quietly to Misha, "You can treat our place as your own, you know. Danute likes to see you around, and even the old girl does, too. It would brighten things up if you came to live with us." He always referred to his wife's rather crazy aunt as "the old girl," but in fact he treated her with more patience and respect than his wife, Danute, ever did.

"We like you, and, in any case, you remind us of Adek."

Adek had been Leon's much younger brother, who had died of typhus shortly before their own son had become infected.

Misha felt both honored and relieved to have such an offer. Now that his mother was dead—dead, actually dead, he had to repeat to himself—the problem of moving could no longer be pushed to the back of his mind. He could never have left the orphanage while she was still alive, he realized that fully only now; the knowledge of her children's relative security under Doctor Korczak's care had been the main comfort of her last weeks. But there was still Rachel! Surely he couldn't desert her just now? I'm all she has left, he thought. He glanced at her pale, frowning face, at her thin legs as she trotted along beside the Doctor, who was reminding her to conserve energy by not walking too fast. But conserving energy was not suited to Rachel's temperament: She does nothing halfheartedly, thought her brother.

Perhaps Leon misunderstood his companion's hesitation, for he said quietly, "Of course, it's a big step, leaving the Orphans' Home. I know you'll not want to make any decision in a hurry. There's no doubt that life would not be as safe with us, Misha."

Misha was embarrassed and suddenly aware of feeling very thirsty. He swallowed hard. "It's not that," he muttered, and then stopped, because perhaps, after all, it *was* just that. He was flattered by the young man's attention and affection but was not really sure how he had earned them. He wasn't to know that, in addition to his pleasant, capable manner and the loyalty and sense of responsibility he'd shown toward his mother, he had other attributes that had impressed Leon and his friends in their youth movement. Those were his comparatively fair complexion and Aryan features, which, in that ghetto summer of 1942, were a potential passport to freedom.

After Mrs. Edelman's funeral Misha found it difficult to settle back into the routine of the orphanage. He became more irritable and very absentminded; twice he dropped dishes while on kitchen duty. In the old days he'd probably have appeared before the Court and been deprived of dessert or honey for a day or two, but by July 1942 such a punishment would have been a mockery. Only the serious crimes, those covered by Paragraphs 900 to 1,000, came before the Court these days. For the most part the children were now too weary, too preoccupied with their hunger and their various ailments, to bother with writing up their more petty complaints against one another.

Once or twice, though, Misha found himself meting out summary—and rough—justice. When he saw Musik, the boy whose mother had run away to be a prostitute, prancing round the courtyard brandishing Abrasha's violin above his head and threatening to smash it, Misha, who was a good deal taller than Musik, stepped in front of him. He grabbed both his wrists, and twisted them into immobility so that Abrasha, his face ashen, his great black eyes—like Joseph's, Misha suddenly saw—almost bursting from their sockets, could retrieve his beloved instrument. He rushed away down to the cellar where the Doctor had cleared a special practice place for him, but Misha did not let the matter rest there. He kicked Musik's bony little backside repeatedly, punishing him for a good deal more than his unkindness to Abrasha. This, he realized later, when he'd calmed down, was exactly the sort of behavior that the Court existed to try and prevent.

Rachel was watching from the kitchen, where she and Halinka, Genia, and Lili were peeling potatoes. When he came in, flushed and tired but oddly elated, she said a little reproachfully, "You went on a bit, Mish. Musik's a lot smaller than you."

"Don't be so prim. Blasted little goody-goody," he snapped back. Of course he hated himself after that: Everything was crumbling now, and with no loving face propped up against worn, gray pillows to tell him otherwise, it began to seem as if his own goodness had been nothing but a bubble of vanity.

The helpers were kind to him, and the Doctor, understanding full well the importance of both attention and privacy to grieving children, tried to spend a little time alone with him and Rachel in the evenings following the funeral. He'd make any excuse, such as asking one or the other or both of them to come up to his room to help him check the height and weight charts, to which he'd always attached so much significance for the purpose of medical research. But starving children, it became apparent to Misha from the stark evidence before him, do not grow much and certainly don't put on weight.

One evening after Rachel had gone to bed, Misha played chess with the Doctor. They both found it difficult to concentrate, but it made Misha especially sad to see how his partner, formerly quite skilled at the game, now had obvious difficulty in considering each move. As he watched him stroke his red beard, his forehead puckered, Misha felt a fresh wave of desire to be in some way worthy of him, and to do some little thing of his own to counteract the misery and wretchedness in which they were all trapped.

One afternoon, about a week after the funeral, Misha went back to Leon's house in Panska Street with more purpose than usual: He intended to broach with Leon his offer of accommodation.

He nodded at the now-familiar group of young mothers sitting on doorsteps around the courtyard. He patted the head of one of the children who ran against him by mistake, and wondered, as he did so often, how and where Eli was at that moment. He stood for a moment watching the children play: The Nazis had with a few exceptions forbidden schools to function, and the group here was therefore one of the many illegal kindergartens that had sprung up all over the ghetto. He made his way up the stairs, remembering the first time he had done so with his breathless but determined mother. This time a Yiddish class was taking place on the first landing. He smiled and gave the boys— younger than himself—a greeting in Yiddish. On the second landing another class was going on, this time a doubly illegal one, for it was a discussion about Polish literature and was being held in Polish. Jews, the Nazis had decided, were no longer to defile the Polish language by daring to use it as their own; and for most Polish Jews, of course, that meant that the use of their mother tongue suddenly became a criminal offense.

Outside Leon's door he paused to regain his breath. His hand raised, he was about to knock when he thought he heard, above the noise of the class downstairs, his own name mentioned. He stood still, his hand in the air; an animated argument was going on in the kitchen, of that there could be no doubt. He distinctly heard Leon's deliberate, rather clipped speech:

"It is too dangerous. Out of the question. He is too young."

"Too *young*. Wake up, Leon! Where have you been for the last two and a half years? When six-year-olds are risking their lives every day to feed their families, then there's no such thing as *too young* anymore."

That, Misha felt sure, was Joseph speaking. Then another, quieter voice, which he didn't recognize, said, "We've plenty of volunteers, Leon, but not many who combine Aryan looks with Misha's obvious dependability."

"But I've no idea what he believes. We've never talked about politics—"

There was a loud thud, as if someone had banged a fist on the table.

"For God's sake, Leon, never mind his *politics*. He's a Jew, isn't he? He wants to survive, doesn't he? Well, we're all Jews and we all want to survive, so we've just got to get on with the job, every one of us, whatever our politics. If it weren't for people like you with your 'ifs' and 'buts' and 'too youngs,' we'd

have had a proper united fighting organization in this ghett
back in March."

Misha was both fascinated and afraid. Half of him wanted t
burst straight in on them and volunteer for whatever had bee
suggested for him. It was the other half, though, that propelle
him, dazed and daunted, back down the overpopulated stai
way. He was in such a hurry to get back to the familiarity of th
orphanage that he literally stumbled through the Yiddish cla
and didn't even acknowledge the young mothers sitting idle o
the courtyard steps.

Just as he arrived back at the kitchen door of the Orphan
Home, Miss Esterka appeared, flushed and out of breath. He
production of Tagore's *Post*, a play about a little boy dying of
serious illness, was to be staged that Saturday, July 18. It was t
be an important affair, involving in at least some small way ev
eryone in the home. Since the day Misha had ventured over t
the other side, the rehearsals had been a welcome diversio
from hunger and sickness.

"Oh, Misha, be a dear and fetch Abrasha for me. I think h
must be practicing in the cellar—he forgets all about time whe
he's there." Abrasha was playing the lead part in the play, so hi
presence at these last rehearsals was essential. Misha stoppe
dead in his tracks and stared at Miss Esterka, whose eyes wer
shining with tension and incipient fever.

"I . . . I . . ." But how could he refuse such a trivial request
How could he admit to lively, talented, overworked Miss Es
terka that he had an overwhelming fear of going into cellars
and had had ever since his best schoolfriend, another Micha
had been buried by rubble together with his family, during th
1939 air raids? But Miss Esterka didn't notice his discomfor
she was already turning away, her mind back with the rehearsa

"Thanks, Misha. And we need you soon for the scen
change," she called over her shoulder.

Misha looked around, already panicky, but there was no sig

of rescue. No one, for once, was working in the kitchen; no one was messing around in the courtyard, either. Always plenty of people around when you need privacy, never anyone when you need them to help, he thought resentfully.

The entrance to the cellar was from the courtyard. He approached the half-open door, and, putting his head just inside, could hear only faint sounds from Abrasha's violin. He knew that Abrasha would be engrossed in his music and that shouting down the stairs wouldn't do the trick. He'd have to go down and fetch him.

"Wretched child," he muttered, clenching his teeth. In fact, Abrasha was scarcely a year younger than Misha. Then he thought of the boy's huge soulful eyes and the grateful way in which he always looked at him since the incident with Musik and the violin, and he felt bad. That wasn't living up to the Doctor's example.

He started gingerly down the narrow stone steps, smelling the damp mustiness of underground places and trying not to think of the other Michal, who had been his close friend since they were about five. Halfway down he tried again. "Abrasha!"

But Abrasha was fiddling away repetitively at some tricky passage, and the call fell on ears that were tuned inward. There was nothing for it: He'd have to go right down into the main part of the cellar—just as Michal and his family must have done under their house—past the all-too-small supply of potato sacks, to where the Doctor had set up a little acetylene stove for the young musician. It was only a matter of about ten to twelve meters, but he looked back and up over his shoulder at least twice to check that the cellar door was still open.

"Abrasha, you're wanted upstairs. Rehearsal time." The boy did look up then, startled, and Misha saw tears glistening in the wide eyes.

"Are you all right?" Misha was torn for the second time in an hour between two strong impulses: the one to beat a hasty retreat from the horrid, low-ceilinged underground room, the other to comfort this shy, appealing boy, who, when he first came to the orphanage after both parents had been killed, hadn't uttered a single word for nearly six months. True to form, Abrasha said nothing now, but he gave Misha the ghost of a smile, put a finger to his lips and then proceeded to play a little melody. It was quite unfamiliar to Misha, who was not musical, anyway, but it spread before him all the sadness of a twelve-year-old child made suddenly alone in the world. Just for a few moments he forgot his unease at being in the cellar and gave the music his full attention, aware that Abrasha was, in his own special way, confiding in him.

CHAPTER 13

THERE WERE STILL TWO days leading up to the performance of the play. Misha was more restless and fidgety than ever, though it had nothing to do with his role as one of the stage crew, which wasn't particularly onerous. He had a good idea that if Leon's friends wanted him for some particular mission, then it probably involved being smuggled over to the Aryan side. So, was his lack of resolve really due to a reluctance to desert Rachel indefinitely? Or did he feel his help at the orphanage was too valuable? Was it shyness that now stopped him from making that short trip back to Panska Street? Or did it have much more to do with a dwindling supply of physical courage?

Then, on the Friday afternoon, while on an errand looking for something in the Doctor's room, he noticed on the desk a list of the people who had been invited to the play. Leon's name was near the top.

That was it! Misha would approach him then, confess that he'd overheard a fragment of conversation about himself, and volunteer for whatever it was they had in mind for him. He couldn't delay any longer. There had been moments enough when he'd vowed to avenge all the wrongs he'd witnessed; the first had been on that April night when he'd seen the baker and his son being shot, and that seemed so very long ago now. The time had come to translate vow into action. But somehow it would be easier to take the plunge here at the orphanage, on home ground.

Saturday came and was greeted by the children with nervous excitement. But, thanks to the now very sick Miss Esterka's tireless efforts, the polished performance was so moving and received so well by the audience that everyone, even those like

Misha whose contribution had been relatively small, shared in the general feeling of elation.

But Misha's share was to be short-lived. Hovering by the makeshift stage waiting to talk to Leon, who was congratulating the Doctor, he heard him ask, "But why, I wonder, did you choose this particular play? It's so sad."

"I would like," replied the Doctor without hesitation, as if he had already had to answer this question in his own mind, "I would like my children to learn how to receive with dignity and peace the Angel of Death."

At that moment Viktor and Sami approached, needing help to move a piece of scenery, so it wasn't until a little later that Misha managed to catch Leon on his own. They walked out of the building together, Leon telling Misha how much he had admired the play.

"I wish Danute had come. But maybe she'd have found it too sad—Abrasha was so convincing as he died at the end." Misha looked at Leon, but all he could see was a dark-winged image of an Angel of Death.

At the entrance to the courtyard they stopped, the orphanage banner flying above them, proud in the failing light.

"I have a confession to make," Misha began shyly. "I overheard you and your friends talking about me, Leon. I'd come to talk about moving into your apartment, but I got scared and—and I just left. I didn't even dare come back later. I'm sorry."

For some reason Misha had expected Leon to be cross, or at least reproachful. In fact, he was nothing of the kind: He was silent for a minute while some other members of the audience left the courtyard, then drew Misha aside, put his hands on the boy's shoulders, and said, in his serious, formal, careful way, "Michal, I am sorry it happened like that. I would like to have prepared you gently. What they want you to do *is* extremely dangerous. But I would be lying to you if I denied that it is also vitally important. Have you heard of liaison workers?"

Misha nodded, dubiously. He thought he'd probably heard the phrase in Leon's own kitchen.

"They are people from the different youth movements—often girls, in fact—who take messages, cash, and false papers to our brothers and sisters cut off in other ghettos and in hiding throughout Poland."

Misha's heart began to beat very fast indeed. "But Leon, how can I . . . I don't . . ."

"You don't know what you could do or how you could do it, I understand that. But you will be trained. There are other young people being trained all the time but—well, we also need more help, all the time." He couldn't bring himself to spell out that this continuous need was due to the high casualty rate among liaison workers.

"Trained? But where? Who by?"

"One of our youth resistance organizations, the Dror, has a group of youngsters—older than you, but not much, I must admit—on a farm near Czerniakow. It's licensed by the Nazis for agricultural work, so you would work in the fields, Michal. The regimen is harsh, too. But the place is, they say, a heaven compared with conditions on this side of the wall. And it serves as a vital safe house for liaisons as well as a meeting place between Jews and the few Poles who risk their lives on our behalf."

"Leon."

"Yes."

"Can I take Rachel with me?"

Leon did not hesitate for a moment.

"No, Michal, you yourself are barely old enough for this work. Rachel would be too obviously young for the farm, and besides . . ."

". . . she looks Jewish." Misha finished for him.

Leon nodded.

"How can I leave her, Leon? I'm the only one she has left."

"She does have the Orphans' Home and the Doctor."

"Whom she shares with nearly two hundred others. God knows, he tries hard enough to share himself out so that there's something for everyone, but, Leon, I'm her *brother,* probably all that's left of her own flesh and blood."

"Michal, I must go now or I shan't be back before curfew. But I must say one thing to you. There are times in life when one has to weigh up a public against a private need. I know I sound pompous—I always have. The others don't really like me because of it. But the choice you have to make is the hardest one for anybody, let alone a boy of not yet fourteen. I want to help you as I would have wanted to help my own brother, but I can't. Not with this. No one else can decide this for you."

Misha stared at the small, earnest, precise young man, prematurely balding and bespectacled. Not unlike the Doctor, in fact, thought Misha, though darker and more strongly built. How on earth, he found himself wondering irrelevantly, did he always manage to look so *tidy?* Even the tear in his shirt had been neatly pinned.

"I suppose," he said eventually, "I suppose I was a Jew before I was Rachel's brother, if you see what I mean."

Leon nodded, and said quickly, "Come the day after tomorrow. There's a meeting at my place at three o'clock. Come then." He turned on his heel, leaving Misha standing under the flag, looking out onto the gray and darkening street and wondering how on earth he was going to tell Rachel of his decision—for he had decided.

The next day a number of the children succumbed to fever, almost as if they'd been willing it to keep away until after the play. Rachel was among the worst affected, and the Doctor had her moved into the sick bay, where he could keep a closer eye on her. Misha hovered around offering to help from time to time, an unvoiced fear in his eyes.

"No, Misha, it's not typhus. Not yet, anyway," the Doctor

reassured him as he handed him some buckets to empty. By some miracle, or rather by the staff's unceasing efforts to maintain high standards of hygiene despite unreliable water supplies, the orphanage had completely escaped the typhus epidemics. But the undernourished children had little or no resistance to the many other virus infections that flourished in the filthy confines of the ghetto. Seeing the Doctor even busier than ever, Misha found it impossible to broach the subject of his departure—it seemed somehow so trivial. Yet he couldn't leave without saying good-bye.

So, the following afternoon, he went to Panska Street as Leon had instructed, but without his little bag of belongings. This time, though plenty of people were sitting around in the building, no organized classes were taking place. This time, too, Leon had left the kitchen door open and welcomed Misha as soon as he appeared on the landing.

Misha looked shyly around the table. No one thought to introduce themselves, but he recognized among them one or two of the young men from other meetings, like big Alexander from downstairs, and sad-eyed Joseph. There was a new man called Yitzhak, who was obviously important because whenever he spoke the others all looked at him attentively, and, sitting beside him, a rather lovely although severe-looking young woman, her fair hair pulled tightly back off her face. He later learned that Tosiah, as she was called, was herself a messenger for the underground, who traveled to ghettos in other cities in order, as she was to put it, "to keep alive the pride, the hope, and the faith." For the moment, though, he was aware only of her penetrating gaze directed upon him.

"You've heard what we want you to do, Michal Edelman. What do you say?" It was the first time Misha had been addressed by his full name since his pre-ghetto school days, and he felt oddly resentful toward her.

"I think I'm ready," he said, almost in a whisper, his throat uncomfortably dry. Standing in the familiar orphanage court-yard the evening before last, it had been comparatively easy to reach a decision; sticking to it was obviously going to be more difficult.

"It's dangerous work, Michal, very dangerous. Have you ever thought that one day you might have to die for your people?"

Misha dumbly shook his head. On the contrary, his thoughts and efforts over the past couple of years had been concentrated exclusively on survival. Of course, every time he'd taken a wallet or a belt to the ghetto wall to exchange for food he'd known he'd been risking his life, but that had been a private, family affair; what he was now being asked to do was altogether different. There had been a relatively simple equation between leather goods and zlotys on the one hand and food and his mother's hold on life on the other; the equation between the taking of a message to some ghetto in Vilna or Lodz and the eventual victory of the Jewish people was a good deal less obvious. Besides, the girl's blue eyes flamed with some quality he didn't altogether trust.

"Of course he hasn't, Tosiah. Don't be so dramatic. He has only just buried his mother," said Leon impatiently, getting up to prepare some tea.

But Tosiah still didn't avert her gaze, and Misha was now filled more with embarrassment than any sense of noble self-sacrifice.

"All the more reason," she said quietly.

Finally, Misha turned to Joseph for help. "How would I get out of the ghetto, please?"

"We take care of that. You'll be provided with papers and you'll join the group that goes each morning to work in a vegetable garden near the Jewish cemetery. As you know, it has a short border with the Christian cemetery."

Misha nodded, frowning. He stared at the middle of the table to avoid meeting anyone's eyes, still unable to fathom quite how, in his little way, he could contribute to the overall fight for his people's survival. The important Yitzhak came to his aid.

"You see, Michal, it's becoming more and more necessary to maintain contact with our brothers and sisters in the camps and ghettos all over Poland."

Misha must still have looked puzzled, for Joseph came in then. "Sometimes that's what we do quite literally," he explained, turning his doleful gaze on the boy. "When families get separated, as they so often do, the news that a brother or a son or a husband is still alive can make the difference between struggling on in one of the labor camps or giving up and dying. We can sometimes supply and deliver false identity papers, too, and that can mean reunion of a mother or father with a child who's hidden in an Aryan family. Then there's cash: A bit of it over the right fence into the right pair of hands can bribe a guard to save a prisoner's life. And all the time we need more and more information—about individuals, about families, about camps, about enemy movements. Do you understand?"

Misha nodded with more assurance now, grateful for the down-to-earth explanation.

"You've left out the most important thing, Joseph," said Tosiah reproachfully. "What about the guns? We need guns and explosives now, Michal, more than anything else. And that means couriers to help keep in contact with the suppliers." Once again Misha was acutely aware of her relentless scrutiny.

Leon put mugs of watery tea on the table and went out to attend to his wife's aunt, who was calling insistently from the next room. Danute herself was not in evidence.

"Do you want to ask anything?" the man Yitzhak asked quietly.

Misha wondered if he dared. He certainly didn't dare lift his mug, knowing that his hand would shake.

Then he said, in a burst, "Yes. Can I take Rachel with me?"

"Now, Michal, you've already asked Leon that and you know in your heart that the answer has to be no."

"Not even to the farm where Leon said I'd be trained?"

The man shook his head. Misha looked around the table at each face in turn: The decision was undoubtedly unanimous. Well, at least he'd given it one last try.

"We hope you'll join us, Misha, but remember that we can't force you."

"If you do," added Joseph, "we can have papers ready for you very soon. You'll need to spend some time in the headquarters in Dzielna Street though, to get to know us, and learn more about the organization."

Leon came back then. Misha said quickly, "Can I go now, please? I'll come back in two days, if that's all right." There was a silence while the others looked at one another.

Then Yitzhak nodded and said, "It's a deal, Misha. Two days."

Leon saw him out onto the landing. "Leon, I would have felt a fool saying this in front of the others. But Rachel has a high fever today—a lot of the children do after the play. I wanted to wait at least until she's a *bit* better. That's why I said two days."

Leon smiled. "Of course, I understand. I have women relatives, too, remember? And, Misha, not a word of this to anyone, not even to the Doctor."

There was no longer any question of having more freedom to decide: Misha's agreement was now taken for granted. But neither of them suspected that the events of the following week would, in any case, eliminate all question of further delay.

CHAPTER 14

AT MIDDAY ON WEDNESDAY, July 22, Doctor Korczak's sixty-fourth birthday, black and white wall posters appeared all over the ghetto announcing that "by order of the authorities, all the Jewish persons living in Warsaw, regardless of age or sex, are to be resettled in the East." There followed a list of categories of people who would for the time being be exempt from deportation, such as those employed by Nazi authorities or firms.

The ghetto that morning had been unusually quiet, eerily empty; even the low, dark clouds overhead seemed to be warning the inhabitants of impending doom. But once the posters *were* in place, the streets began to fill with people who crowded around them, first in silence, later in a babble of speculation. What did it all really mean? Why should it be only the weakest, least productive members of the population who had to go, like mothers with young children? And where exactly were they going? And, most important, how to get hold of an official document to "prove" that one was exempt from evacuation? It might be hell in the confines of the ghetto, but a hell you knew was certainly preferable to the terrors of the unknown.

Misha and the other children in the sanctuary of the Orphans' Home were to some extent cocooned from this early panic. But not for long. The last paragraph of the deportation decree demanded that the hospital in Stawki Street be turned into an assembly point for six thousand Jews every day. Consequently the hospital had to be emptied of all its patients immediately. The very next day, eighty-five of the sickly, starving children in the hospital were transferred to the Orphans' Home: Space and sustenance had to be found for them somehow.

Rachel was over the worst of her fever by now and back in

her own bed, though still far from well. With many of the less ill children having to double up and share beds, and with six more cots squeezed into the Doctor's already-cramped isolation room, Misha saw that the time had unmistakably come. He could do no other than take up the offer of Leon's roof and the dangerous challenge that went with it.

After packing his few things together, Misha went in search of the Doctor. He was in the lavatories emptying buckets of urine. Misha told him in a few garbled words that he had been offered lodgings at Leon's house. For a long moment Korczak looked up at the boy he thought of as a grandson and then said, "Michal, you don't have to go. You know that, don't you?"

"The time has come, Mister Doctor. And I'll come back to help you and see Rachel as often as I can."

The Doctor put down the buckets with a clank. He stood up slowly and with obvious discomfort, wiped his glasses on his green apron, and said, "Then you must memorize Elena's address. I don't want to write it down anywhere. Now repeat after me. . . ." After two repetitions the name and address of Elena's foster parents were engraved on Misha's mind. Then, unsure how to take his leave of the Doctor, Misha bent down and carried the three empty buckets back up to the sick room for him. Once there, he heard Julek calling out in a tearful voice, probably frightened by a fitful dream; Misha didn't wait around, for he could see that Doctor Korczak had more than enough on his hands. After all, this wasn't really good-bye—he'd be back often enough. He must see Rachel before he left, though.

"I'll come and see you as often as I can—like Hanka comes to see Nussen," Misha told his sister. He wanted to reassure her with "every day," but knew it would be quite wrong to make rash promises. "And Rachel," he warned timidly, "if I don't turn up for a while, it doesn't mean I've forgotten you. I expect there'll be things I'll have to do."

Rachel narrowed her dark eyes and watched him carefully.

She knew him well enough to suspect he was keeping something from her, but she had neither the will nor the energy to nag it out of him as she might once have done.

There was no privacy at all in the orphanage now, so they walked out into the courtyard together. The weather was still and humid and overcast, and the flag at the gate hung limp.

"Misha, would you think it very silly if we said a prayer together, before you go?"

"Of course not." Misha's heart was very full, and he was quite oblivious to the soccer game going on in the courtyard. Quietly, with two fingers linked and without consultation, they recited two prayers: One was their favorite from the Doctor's book of *Prayers for People Who Do Not Pray*; the other, taught them by their father, was an echo from a lost world.

For a few days Misha managed to make visits from Panska Street back to the orphanage and made himself useful fetching and carrying for the Doctor and Mrs. Stefa and the others. But as Operation Reinhard—as the deportation plan was called—progressed, the geography of the ghetto was transformed, and venturing out anywhere became more and more hazardous. Because people employed in Nazi enterprises were, to begin with, exempt from resettlement, wooden fences were erected around all the factories and workshops, so that the ghetto became in effect a collection of little fenced-in ghettos, quite isolated from one another. The youth movement to which Leon and his friends belonged had its headquarters in Dzielna Street, and Leon and Misha established a routine of leaving Panska Street early in the morning—like early evening, the safest time of day—and spending the time up in Dzielna Street until the day's trainloads had left.

One of the main activities at the headquarters was the frantic production of "livelihood cards"—false permits—which "proved" that the person named and pictured was a genuine employee of a Nazi-run business and therefore exempt from deportation. Misha was entrusted with the task of distributing these permits to the nearer destinations and then, before the end of the first week, he was given a pile of handbills to paste up at the entrances to tenement blocks and other buildings. The bills contained a clear message to the Jewish public, informing them that resettlement meant Treblinka, and Treblinka meant death, and urging them therefore to hide and resist.

One afternoon a young woman tackled Misha as he pasted a bill in the entrance to her building.

"That's just scaremongering," she said angrily as she read the notice. "People are only being taken to workcamps. Why should they offer us all those kilos of bread and jam to volunteer for resettlement if they only mean to kill us? That'd be a stupid waste. Anyway, my friend has had a card from her father to say he's all right where they've taken him."

Misha didn't know how to reply. She had by the hand a little barefoot boy not much bigger than Eli. He looked into her eyes and saw the fear, and understood how vital it was for her to believe that the Nazi bait of bread and jam did actually promise a future. Shivering, despite the heat, he thought of Mister Doctor and the children back at the orphanage, and prayed to his unnamed God that they were safe. The thing inside him moved again, but only feebly now.

As he finished sticking up his supply of handbills, Misha reflected on how odd it was that, though lots of people said they'd received postcards from resettled relatives, it seemed impossible actually to get a glimpse of one. As with ghosts, it was always someone else who'd seen one.

His errand took him up to the corner with Gesia Street, and it was there that he suddenly heard a bloodcurdling scream, followed by wailing, shouts, and sporadic rifle fire. He knew instinctively and exactly what the sounds meant. He had no wish to witness one of those horrifying roundups, so he wasted no time in getting back to headquarters, where news of the dreadful happenings in Gesia Street had already preceded him. Leon, who was already extremely anxious about the daily trips right across the ghetto to and from Panska Street and who tried every day to find a nearer room for himself and his dependants, put his foot down after this first of the late afternoon roundups, and refused to take Misha home with him that evening.

"Joseph will be here with you. You'll have to bed down on a pile of newspapers, but it's safer, Misha, much safer."

"But Rachel—I told her—"

"Rachel will understand. I'll get a message to the orphanage for you if I don't go myself. You can write a note if you like."

Misha knew Leon was right. Rachel would understand, for on his last visit two or three days before she had said to him anxiously, "Hanka has told me what it's like out there now. I know people are being beaten and shot and rounded up and taken away. It's too dangerous for you to be out on the streets, Misha."

"Hanka visits Nussen every day," he had objected.

"That's different. Nussen is all Hanka has left. But we still have Eli, and for her sake, wherever she is, you must stop taking unnecessary risks." Misha had even smiled at this vestige of his sister's bossiness—in happier days he used to accuse her of being a prig and a know-it-all, but there was a part of him now that was only too glad to be bossed.

"Besides," she had added with unconcealed pride, "I don't think Hanka is needed in the way you are."

She doesn't miss much, Misha thought, aware that she had put two and two together. He realized now that with Leon's instructions added to hers he would have to do as he was told.

Days passed, and Misha heard nothing more about the plan to smuggle him out of the ghetto. But everyone was so rushed and preoccupied that he didn't like to ask about it: He assumed that with the sudden demand for "livelihood cards" his own papers had simply taken lower priority. He himself was kept very busy. He ran errands as far as Mila Street, where there was another important center of underground activity, took part in Hebrew classes, helped serve in the children's soup kitchen, and generally made himself useful. He felt very much a part of the new concerted struggle against the enemy and shared the spirit of desperate elation that it generated among those who worked in the Fighting Organization. He came to know by sight a lot of people, both in his own youth movement and other allied ones, but although they greeted him in a friendly way, they were all too busy to stop and talk, and Misha knew moments of acute loneliness. Leon was unfailingly kind to him, but in his characteristically polite, precise way, and Misha found himself missing the easy informality of the Orphans' Home. In any case, Leon's skills as a printer were in great demand, and, with his responsibilities in Panska Street as well, he was unable to spend much time with his young protégé. Misha certainly didn't feel he could talk to him about the misgivings, which played havoc with his stomach every time he imagined making his way through Nazi-patrolled Poland to ghettos in distant towns.

At least fear takes the edge off hunger, he thought with a wry smile, as he settled down one evening on his bed of newspapers in one of the storerooms at Dzielna Street. Joseph, who had a similar berth in another corner, had just offered him some soup, and, to Misha's own amazement, he had actually turned it down.

Then, on August 5, they broke the news to him that was to scatter those unvoiced fears and misgivings like a great ugly scarecrow. Some other Dror members had been shot while escaping via the vegetable garden route, and it was therefore considered no longer safe.

"How, then—?"

"There's only one way that is reasonably safe, Michal, and it's not very pleasant."

Misha sat back on the pile of newspapers that had become his bed. He looked up at Leon, his mouth suddenly emptied of saliva. Sheer physical panic seized him, beginning in his feet and rising up like an electric current through his limbs. "Not . . . not the sewers?" he croaked.

"Michal, it's the safest way. There are some excellent guides—why, like young Adziu from the orphanage. He's taken lots of people out to safety. He knows those tunnels like the back of his hand."

Misha said nothing. He saw Leon's lips moving in a sort of blur.

"It'll be dark and wet and smelly, Michal, but it's the safest way, and in twenty minutes you'll be out in Saxon Park."

Dark and wet and smelly, dark and wet and smelly reeled through Misha's head like a record stuck in a groove. If only he could explain that it wasn't the dark, the wet, or the smells that filled him with dread. All those were minor discomforts in comparison with the idea of being cramped, caught, crushed beneath that vast weight of concrete above. There was no way he could make Leon understand. How could he *show* him the state of his stomach? How could he talk with a dried-out throat? It was so *shaming*. Boys as young and younger than he, boys like Adziu, were volunteering to spend hours at a time guiding people around the network of city sewers, and here he was, terrified of venturing into them once for a twenty-minute trip.

He slept scarcely at all that night, tossing and turning on the improvised mattress. Once he gave way to silent sobs, feeling the warm wetness turn to mush beneath him. Never in his life had he felt so alone. Joseph and two other young men were whispering among themselves in the dark about the wording of a new handbill, and although Misha knew he ought to be interested, all he really wanted was someone to talk to about his own private fears. Perhaps for the very first time since her death he realized how much he missed his mother.

He owed it to her memory, and that of his father, not to mention the Doctor and Rachel and Eli and all the others, to conquer his terror and go out and work for the resistance beyond the ghetto walls, where it might not yet be too late to have some effect. But this one thing they had now asked him to do—that was impossible. There were, after all, limits to the powers of endurance of a fourteen-year-old boy. Adziu must have his own limits, different ones maybe, but he must have them. It couldn't be just he, Misha, who had been tested and found wanting. He clenched his fists, his face buried in his trousers, which he used as a pillow, thinking of all the other times in recent months when he had been found wanting. Perhaps, after all, it was better that he should be alone and that the people he most loved and respected should not be there to witness his humiliation. Rachel, damn her, would have accepted the challenge without hesitation.

When the whispered consultation was over, Joseph heard the boy moving around restlessly. He guessed something, but only something, of his private anguish and called softly across. "All right, Michal?"

"All right, Joseph, thanks. G'night." He'd keep it to himself if it killed him.

As if to underline the darkness in Misha's heart, August 6 dawned clear and bright; high above the ghetto walls the sky was a radiant blue. But down below the heat soon became intense and muggy, and by noon the temperature had risen to eighty-four degrees. That morning Misha was detailed off to the "shop" on the corner of Mila Street to help one of the reporters working for the underground press. He was sorting piles of mimeographed papers when he heard the now-familiar cacophony of deportees being driven and beaten along like so many cattle. He worked faster, as if thereby to shut out the sounds of misery that penetrated the brick walls.

Then suddenly there was a cry. "Oh, my God, it's Korczak and the children!"

It came from another helper, someone who might not have known of Misha's connection with the orphanage. Several other people rushed to peer out of the windows, taking care nevertheless to stand well back and to the side, for it was not uncommon for guards to take potshots at people impudent enough to peek out at the evacuations.

Misha pushed his way to the front, careless of his own safety. Someone pulled him firmly back, but he could still see all he needed to see. There was no mistake: It was indeed Korczak and the children.

They made up only a small part of the crowd of four to five thousand people who were being beaten and shoved along the street to the assembly place, about a hundred meters from where Misha was standing. Yet instead of merging into the throng, they somehow stood out as different and separate. Whereas other people were tripping and falling over one another and over luggage and personal belongings that spilled out across the street, Korczak's group seemed to remain upright and intact, marching with slow dignity.

At the head of the column Misha saw the old Doctor, the man who had been both his guardian and his friend, defiantly without arm band as always, but now also without his glasses. He was carrying one of the younger children, whose face was turned away. Misha leaned forward to get a better view—it could have been Romcia, but he wasn't sure; and a little boy—yes, Nussen it was—walked by his side holding his hand. Beside them, upright and proud as ever, Musik carried the orphanage flag, the blue Star of David toward Misha, bright against its white background. By contrast the stars on the children's arm bands were a sullen gold in the glare of the sun.

There was Abrasha, struggling along exhausted between Sami and Viktor, his violin clutched under one arm. I want my children to receive with dignity. . . , thought Misha, as he picked out row upon row of familiar faces. The children's wooden shoes beat out a dirge as they trudged slowly along in the midday heat. With a wild surge of hope Misha prayed, as the extraordinary procession passed four or five abreast beneath his gaze, that Rachel would somehow not be there.

But of course she was there. Right at the end of the line, carrying one of the new tiny tots from the hospital. She walked wearily between her friend Genia and Mrs. Stefa, who wore her familiar faded, shapeless jumper. Misha saw his sister only for a moment; she was soon obscured by the bulky figure of one of the guards.

And so, dry-eyed and unprotesting, Misha simply watched as all that was dear and familiar to him marched out of his life forever. For none of the onlookers in that suddenly silent room had any illusions about "resettlement in the East." Their couriers had told them exactly what awaited the freight cars that left Warsaw daily with their human cargo.

The children passed, but the silence in the room remained. One young man gently took hold of Misha's arm and led him to a corner where they sat down, their backs against the wall. Misha shook his head continuously; eventually he whispered from a throat once again bone dry, "They've gone. They've *all* gone." Ben, the young man, just nodded and patted his shoulder, for there really was nothing to add: He himself was the only survivor of his family.

At that moment Leon rushed into the room, red-faced and out of breath, disheveled as Misha had never seen him before. "Korczak and the children. Did you see them?" he gasped.

Then he caught sight of Misha, white-faced and staring, and went to squat down beside him. He found nothing to say. Misha looked at him, now strangely clearheaded and calm, and said, "I'm ready to go, even if it means the sewers. But Adziu won't be able to guide me now, will he?"

CHAPTER 15

LEON, RECOGNIZING MISHA'S new resolve but fearing that it might be short-lived, soon disappeared again to ensure that his false Aryan papers be given top priority and to make arrangements for another sewer guide. Meanwhile, Misha remained at the "shop" in Mila Street and continued to sort papers, his movements mechanical, his mind mercifully numb.

Back at the Dror headquarters in Dzielna Street early that evening, Misha began to doubt his own sanity when Adziu himself walked into the room and greeted him casually as if he'd just been for a Sunday stroll. Adziu, he learned, was the only child who had actually been in the building at the time of the evacuation and survived. He had simply hidden behind the bathroom door with a bayonet.

This bayonet was to Adziu what the violin had been to Abrasha; it was a relic from his days with the partisans in the forests, whom he'd joined when he jumped from one of the early trains deporting Jews to camps in the East. His mother had bribed a guard with her diamond engagement ring to look the other way while her son and daughter jumped. Adziu was to bear forever both the facial and the emotional scars of that leap; even now he seldom passed an adult woman without scanning her features eagerly, just in case his mother should have returned. But now, once again, his life was saved as if by a miracle. He held the bayonet—which had lived under his mattress since he came to the orphanage—against the throat of the Jewish policeman who had gone around the building checking for stragglers. The policeman had shouted down "All clear" and then hastened down himself, under orders. Immediately afterward, as the building fell prey to looters, Adziu hid the bayonet in his trousers, mingled with the crowd, and disappeared.

Misha was in a way pleased to see him, but a voice somewhere inside him whispered, "Why Adziu, why not Rachel?" He didn't want to hear any more about those last moments at the orphanage, so he didn't ask any questions.

But Adziu, not normally the type of boy to volunteer information, had one more piece of news he wanted to share with Misha.

"They are saying that at the Umschlagplatz the guards told Mister Doctor he could stay behind, and he refused. Amazing, isn't it?"

There was a moment's silence while Adziu waited for Misha's agreement. Then, slowly, Misha replied, "No, I don't really think it is amazing. Not amazing, knowing Mister Doctor. I reckon he made that decision a long time ago—he couldn't let the children go without him now."

Absurdly he was relieved that the Doctor had indeed gone with them, almost as if, by so doing, he had ensured Rachel's safety for a few hours longer.

Adziu shrugged, and his face became more puckered than usual in a frown of bewilderment. Then he changed the subject abruptly. "Anyway, I hear they're sending you out through the sewers tonight. Since I'm still here, they've asked me to take you. No need to worry. I know them well." Adziu had learned the safest routes in another phase of his charmed life: He had worked for three months with one of the ghetto's big-time smugglers, between arriving in Warsaw and being rescued by Doctor Korczak from a severe beating in the street.

"We'll meet at ten o'clock. Hide just inside the doorway of the house on the corner with Karmelicka. That will give us plenty of time—you're being met across the river from Saxon Park at midnight."

Misha went back to his little corner between the filing cabinets in the storeroom. Apart from his family photographs, which he packed carefully in some old handbills, clean sides against the pictures, before tucking them into his grubby shirt pocket, there was nothing else he wanted to take with him. Rachel, like the other children, had been carrying a small bundle under her free arm. Much good her things will be where she is now, he thought bitterly. He looked across the curfew-quiet street from the patched-up mosaic of window, and sent a fervent prayer to Rachel out across the miles. Whether or not they still shared the same world, she would somehow hear and know—that much at least he could still hope.

The one thing that Misha did take with him in abundance were the good wishes of Leon and the other members of the Dror movement. He was aware that the deportation of Korczak and the children seemed to have put him in a sort of limelight; even severe Tosiah and the man called Yitzhak came to say good-bye. Then Leon accompanied him down the street to the rendezvous with Adziu, formally he shook his hand, and whispered, "Good-bye, young brother, and may God go with you."

"Good-bye, Leon, and thank you for every . . ." but the small, shy man had already turned away. In the pale moonlight Misha saw one hand lifted in farewell.

At the corner of Karmelicka and Leszno streets the two boys froze at the sound of boots patrolling somewhere behind them. As they hugged the doorway of a leather tannery, motionless in deep shadow, the patrol passed by within meters, twenty guns ready to shoot.

"We're waiting for a signal," explained Adziu in a whisper, after they'd gone. Misha nodded and shivered. He wore his two old patched sweaters one on top of the other, and the night wasn't cold, but all the same he knew his skin was goose-pimply. He patted the special pocket with his brand-new Aryan papers in their protective covering.

Suddenly Adziu nudged Misha and spat out, "Now!" He dashed for a manhole cover in the middle of the street, leaned down to lever it up with a fragment of metal, and slid it almost noiselessly back onto the cobblestones. He beckoned Misha impatiently and gestured into the uncovered hole. Misha gulped, and his heart raced, but he had no time to hesitate. Almost before he realized what was happening, he was clambering backward down a wet, sticky ladder. Well before he reached the bottom, he heard the squeal of vermin; he shuddered involuntarily and felt himself begin to slip. He gripped harder and took some comfort at the sight of Adziu's pale feet coming down above him in the blackness. When they reached the bottom, he felt the cold, foul sewage seep into his shoes and up inside his trouser bottoms. Adziu whispered, "Keep your face as close to the water as possible—the gas is better there. If you have to be sick, for God's sake be quiet about it—noise carries along these tunnels. Just tug, and I'll stop."

Adziu dropped to his knees, and Misha did likewise. They entered a tunnel not more than one and a half meters high and only just wide enough for one person at a time. Misha felt his shoulders scrape the roof; he grabbed the tail of Adziu's shirt and crammed it into his mouth, biting down hard. This left both his hands free to support himself against the sides of the tunnel, and for some obscure reason it also prevented the panic, which throbbed everywhere in his body, from taking total control over him. But it didn't help the tides of nausea in his stomach and chest. The stench was overwhelming, and once or twice he slipped, so that the vile ooze actually penetrated his nose and throat. At one point he tugged hard on Adziu's shirttail to make him stop while he turned sideways to vomit. But even while he was retching and vomiting, he gripped onto the shirt with one hand, so terrified was he of becoming separated from his guide.

After what seemed an endless time, they emerged from the maze of narrow tunnels and found themselves shoulder deep in the fast waters of a main sewer. Misha could hear rats swimming past, squealing in the darkness, and his stomach contracted again, this time in a massive convulsion. The fumes in the main sewer were even thicker, and, succumbing to dizziness, Misha was utterly convinced he was about to die. Thank goodness, he thought, that Rachel had not been subjected to such a death as this. But he didn't quite give up, for he transferred Adziu's shirt to both hands now and continued to clutch at the material as if at life itself.

By the time they reached their destination, Misha had lost all sense of time. He was aware of Adziu pushing him out of the stream and against a wall. "We've arrived," he whispered. He placed Misha's hands firmly on the sides of a ladder and hissed, "G'luck." Dazed as if drunk, Misha straightened up and mechanically began to climb the slimy rungs, dimly aware of pinpricks of light above him. At the top, he jabbed at the manhole cover with one hand, enough to lift it a few centimeters and to get a lungful of fresh night air. He replaced the cover and then, more gently this time, lifted it from the opposite lip; very gingerly he repeated the operation three times, terrified of losing his balance on the slippery ladder, before being certain that no one was in sight. He wasn't even sure that he cared very much now; surely capture by the Nazis would be preferable to another trip through Hell. But the coast was clear: A mere seven or eight meters away was a fountain he recognized. He was, unbelievably, in Saxon Park in Aryan Warsaw.

As he half walked, half reeled away from the manhole, he heard the soft scrape of the cover being slid back into place by Adziu. Adziu, thought Misha, how long can it have taken you to get so familiar with that dreadful underworld? He regretted not having made more of an effort to get to know the strange foxy-faced boy with the two livid scars; he might not have been particularly easy to talk to, but he had more than his fair share of guts.

Misha's shoes sloshed vile-smelling ooze. Looking furtively around him, he stopped just once to empty them.

Breathing the cool air in large greedy gulps, he walked

quickly down to the grassy bank of the Vistula and headed for the first bridge that crossed the river into the well-to-do suburb of Praga. Still dazed and nauseous, he longed to stop and wash out his stinking clothes in the darkly gleaming water, but dared not delay for a minute, having lost all sense of time while down in the sewers.

He was halfway across the bridge before he realized just what an easy target he would make from either bank, exposed there in the moonlight. He stopped uncertainly, surprised, after everything that had happened, still to be capable of feeling fear. Then, hearing the sound of a distant train, he squelched quickly onward.

As he approached the rendezvous beside the railway tracks, a dark figure emerged from the shadows of a hut. Misha hesitated again, his heart drumming.

"Orphans' Home!" came the whispered signal, and Misha stumbled eagerly forward into the stranger's embrace.

POSTSCRIPT

JANUSZ KORCZAK

JANUSZ KORCZAK, WHOSE real name was Henryk Goldszmit (he adopted his non-Jewish pen name at the age of twenty, when submitting a prize-winning play for a competition, and kept it throughout his life), was born in Warsaw on July 22, 1878, or possibly 1879, for his father was late in registering his birth, probably to try and delay his son's being conscripted into the army when he grew up. Both his father, a successful lawyer, and his grandfather, a doctor, did much to bridge the gap of ignorance and mistrust that divided Poles from Jews, and consequently the family was well integrated into Polish life and culture.

But Korczak was only five when he had his first encounter with anti-Semitism. Burying his pet canary in a candy tin, he was teased by his playmate, the son of the building's concierge, who told him that like all Jews, Korczak's canary had no soul and would go to hell. The boy went on to suggest that a sufficient supply of candy paid over to him might ensure Korczak's own escape from damnation!

When Korczak was eleven, his father became mentally ill and later, as a consequence, bankrupt. While still a schoolboy, Korczak helped to support his mother and sister by giving extra tutoring to the children of wealthy friends and acquaintances in his spare time. He went on to train as a doctor at Warsaw University and worked as a pediatrician for seven years, before taking over his first orphanage in 1911. In making the decision to change direction in this way, he knowingly abandoned all material benefits associated with the career of a successful doctor, and dedicated himself to improving the lot of a large number of homeless and destitute children, whose hardships he would share until his death.

Children, whether Jewish or Christian, were to Korczak the most important thing in life, and it was only in later years that he devoted himself exclusively to Jewish children. He never married—there was speculation that he was afraid of passing on the mental illness that had afflicted his father if he had a family of his own—but his commitment to his young charges was total.

Far more than a head of home and administrator, Korczak was also a teacher, scientist, writer of classic children's stories and plays, fund-raiser, commentator on social welfare, physician, educational theorist—and, in the 1930s, a much-loved radio broadcaster on matters relating to children. He was very much ahead of his time in his theories, which had as their core "the right of the child to respect." He believed in the "absolute, complete value of the child as human being of the present—not the future," and his life's work reflected this fundamental belief. No task was too lowly or menial for him to perform for his children; he would shave the hair of newcomers and cut toenails with the same care and attention as for thirty years he put into writing the editorial in the weekly *Orphanage Gazette*.

Though unfailingly gentle with his children, Korczak could be a tough and defiant advocate on their behalf. During times of particular hardship, and especially after the outbreak of war in 1939, he did not flinch from begging and, if necessary, shaming affluent citizens into making donations toward the children's welfare. It was entirely in character that, when the orphanage was being moved into the ghetto in November 1940 and a truckload of potatoes was confiscated by the Nazis, he immediately went to the Gestapo Headquarters to demand its return. He was badly beaten up and thrown into the notoriously severe Pawiak Prison, where he remained for the next four weeks, until bought out by three of his ex-pupils.

During his absence that winter, Mrs. Stefa continued to run the orphanage as faithfully and efficiently as she had more than twenty-five years before, when Korczak had been away at the front with the army's Medical Corps during the First World War. Stefania Wilczynska—Mrs. Stefa's real name—was herself from a wealthy Jewish-Polish background, and had denied herself a comfortable material existence in order to share Korczak's work for the underprivileged children of Warsaw.

It was while away from the orphanage at the Eastern Front, working in the appalling conditions of front-line military hospitals, that Korczak worked out the Code of Laws for his Children's Court. "The Court," he wrote, "must defend the timid against the bullies, the conscientious against the careless and idle." Korczak wanted his children to understand the idea of justice, and of just and unjust laws. "The Court," says the Preamble to the Code, "is not justice, but it should strive for justice. The Court is not truth, but its goal is truth. Judges may make mistakes. . . . But it is shameful if a judge consciously hands down an unjust verdict." At the beginning of every Saturday Court session, he would ask, "No one has been hit by the staff. True or not?" There appears to be no record of any adult having struck a child in one of Korczak's orphanages.

In the 1930s, Korczak made two visits to Palestine. He was never a religious man in the orthodox sense; yet, deeply depressed by the growing anti-Semitism in Poland, he cherished a dream of one day being able to retire to the Promised Land. But once the Nazis had invaded Poland on September 1, 1939, he knew that his dream would never be realized. Writing to friends in Palestine he said, "If I left, I would never forgive myself. I detest desertion. My vocabulary does not allow it. So be it!" And later, in 1942, when a loyal Aryan friend came to visit him disguised as a water and sewer inspector and armed with false identity papers to enable Korczak to escape through the ghetto wall as a locksmith, he received a similar response.

This attitude was clearly something the Nazi authorities did not understand when, on August 6, 1942, concerned that his martyrdom might rally resistance in the ghetto, they responded to a plea from a Jewish intermediary and sent a messenger through the panic-stricken crowds waiting for deportation on the sweltering Umschlagplatz, to deliver to Korczak a letter of reprieve. No one knows what Korczak's words were on receiving this message, but it is not hard to guess their gist. An eyewitness reports that "Korczak entered the freight car first, followed by the youngest children. Mrs. Stefa and the rest went into the next car." The exact time and details of the death of Korczak and the children are not known, but on the day of their deportation to Treblinka, August 6, it is known that over ten thousand people were exterminated there.

Misha and his family are entirely fictional; but, in addition to Mister Doctor and Mrs. Stefa, many of the characters in this book, including the orphanage helpers, are based on historical people. Musik was the illegitimate child of a Polish prostitute, who waited for three days for his mother to return after she had left him to go and work in a German officers' brothel. Eventually, he took himself to the orphanage, where he fainted from hunger as he waited at the door.

Abrasha's parents were killed by the SS, and he was brought to the orphanage by his aunt. He took his violin everywhere, even to the lavatory, and one day was teased by Musik, who threatened to steal and break the instrument. It was Halinka, one of the girls who does not feature largely in my story, who came to Abrasha's rescue and earned his unswerving devotion. After the death of his parents he had neither spoken a word nor played a note on the violin for nearly six months, and it was this incident and ensuing gratitude that helped him to break his long silence. And Mister Doctor really did find Abrasha a place in the potato cellar where he could practice in private.

Finally, Adziu was sewer guide in real life as in this book. In 1938, on one of the early deportation trains, Adziu's mother did manage to bribe a guard to look the other way while her son and daughter jumped. Adziu was quite badly injured in the leap but was found and treated by partisans, with whom he and his sister lived for a year in the mountains of southeastern Poland. While with them he had to do many brutal things that were to leave scars as deep as those caused by his jump. On one occasion he was given the "privilege" of pushing the handle on a detonator, thus blowing up a German troop train. He was twelve at the time.

Eventually, when the partisans disbanded, Adziu left his sister in the care of one of them and managed to make his way to Warsaw, where he lived by begging and smuggling via the sewer routes. Doctor Korczak rescued him from a beating in the street and took him to the orphanage, where he kept his bayonet hidden under the mattress. And Adziu was the only child in the orphanage building to escape evacuation by hiding behind a door and then threatening the guard with his bayonet.

If these stories of horror and love have one message for those of us who live in happier circumstances, it is, surely, one of humility; for none of us can know the limits—good or evil, moral or physical—of which we are capable, until put to the test.

—C.L.

ACKNOWLEDGMENTS

I HAVE READ MANY memoirs and diaries in the preparation of this novel, but would like to acknowledge a specific debt to: *Mister Doctor* by Hanna Olczak, translated by Roald Jan Kruk and Harold Gresswell (Peter Davies, 1985), until recently the only biography of Doctor Korczak in English; and particularly *A Field of Buttercups* by Joseph Hyams (Frederick Muller, 1969). A much fuller biography in English has now been published and was of help in the final editing stages of this novel. It is: *The King of Children* by Betty Jean Lifton (Chatto, 1988; Farrar, Straus & Giroux, 1988).